# INSPIRING YOU

*(Unraveling You, #4)*

## JESSICA SORENSEN

For information: jessicasorensen.com
ISBN: 978-1511750912

Cover design by MaeIDesign

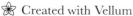 Created with Vellum

# Ayden

❦

*S*omething inside me
    *Guides me down a desolate road.*
    *Leading to somewhere.*
*Leading into the unknown.*
*Nothing but darkness.*
*All, all alone.*
*Terrified to be found.*
*Fucking fearing the end.*
*Still, I make my way down that road.*
*Clutching onto the hope*
*Of reaching you one day.*
*It's all I have to hold onto*
*Until I get to you again.*

"Hey, can we talk for a minute?" Lila, my adoptive mother, asks as she sticks her head into my room.

"Yeah, sure." I close the notebook that I scribble my thoughts and lyrics into. "Is something wrong?" I ask as I scoot to the edge of my bed and lower my feet to the floor.

She shakes her head as she walks into my room. "No,

honey. Nothing's wrong. I just want to talk." She sits down beside me. "You've seemed kind of quiet at dinner lately, and with everything going on..." She sighs. "I just want to make sure you're doing okay with everything."

"I'm fine," I say, hoping I don't sound as guilty as I feel.

The truth is, a ton of shit is wrong, more than she realizes. Not only have the police found no new information on where my sister, Sadie, is, but I also have an officer following me around twenty-four seven. While I'm grateful they're protecting me, I'm not sure what the hell I'm going to do when Monday rolls around, and I have to go to my therapy appointment. Hopefully, I can think of a good excuse as to why I'm going to a doctor's office; otherwise, I won't be able to go through with my plan.

"I know but..." Lila mulls something over while staring out the window where the stars and moon have taken over the sky. "You just seem a little different lately." She looks at me, worry lines creasing her eyes. "Ethan and I are worried you might be holding stuff in, especially after you found out about your dad... And that letter you got the other day..." She shudders. "I know it has to be hard for you."

The letter that arrived in the mail the other day was addressed to me. Fiona was the one who collected it from the mailbox. Thankfully, Lila got a hold of it before anyone else did, noted the lack of a return address, and handed it over to the police. While I don't know what the contents of the letter are, I've noticed I'm being watched more closely, so I'm guessing it was another threat.

"Sweetie, I just want you to know we're not going to let anything happen to you." Lila pats my leg. "Your father... these people... they're not going to get ahold of you."

I do my best not to think about the father I never knew,

and if he really is part of the evil group who once kidnapped my siblings and me and who still has my sister. Because, if I think about him too much, then I start thinking about *everything*. And the more I analyze every-thing, the more I get dragged back into the darkness I let own me for too long. And I don't want to be stuck in the darkness anymore. I realized that when a member of the Soulless Mileas lured me into the woods. I thought I was going to die out there in the dark, by myself, haunted by my fears I never overcame. When I didn't die, I promised myself *no more being afraid*.

*No more fear.*
*Only fight.*
*Forever and ever.*
*No matter what*
*I'll fight until the end.*

Lila sighs at my silence, her shoulders slumping forward with disappointment. "Are you sure there isn't anything you want to tell me?"

My stomach twists with guilt. *It's like she knows what I'm going to do.*

I shake my head. No, if she knew what I was up to, she'd put a stop to it. "I'm okay. I promise. I'm just a little caught up with graduating and stuff. There's a lot going on."

She smiles. "I still can't believe you'll be a high school graduate in just a few days. It seems like only yesterday we were bringing you home."

"Two years has gone by kind of fast, hasn't it?" I realize the truth of my words.

With all of this crazy shit going on with the Soulless Mileas, I haven't had time to step back and think about how quickly time flies. In just a few days, I'll be out of high school, and I have no clue what I want to do. Most of my time has been spent trying to find my brother and sister. My search for my brother ended painfully with the police finding his body near my old childhood home. They believe the Soulless Mileas played a role in his death, but since they can't track down any of the members, no one has paid for taking his life.

"It has gone by pretty fast. Too fast, at least for me." Her eyes tear up, and she unexpectedly throws her arms around me. "I'm so proud of you. You're such a strong, good person, Ayden. I'm so lucky I get to have you as my son."

I pat her back, not feeling as uncomfortable as I used to when she hugged me, but hugging is still out of my comfort zone. "Thank you … For saying that. It means a lot to me."

"I'm just saying the truth. You're an amazing person, Ayden Gregory."

I wonder how my graduation conversation would've went if my birth mother hadn't handed us over to those horrible people, if she were still alive, and my brother and sister and I were living with her. Would I even be graduating? Would I have ever truly felt what it was like to be loved and taken care of? I want to say yes. I want to believe my life with her wasn't all bad. And maybe it wasn't. There were some good moments that the four of us shared, but most of the good was lost in a sea of yelling, abuse, and neglect.

By the time Lila and I pull away from the hug, my eyes are burning with tears. I don't want to cry. I've been doing too much of that lately in the privacy of my room, whenever I think too much or when I have a nightmare about the past.

Lila dabs her eyes with her fingertips, wiping away smeared makeup. "Well, I just want you to know I'm here if you ever need to talk."

"I know," I say. "And I appreciate that, but I promise I'm just a little distracted by school and stuff."

"All right." She rises to her feet and reluctantly leaves the room.

The moment she shuts the door, I grab my pen and notebook and get out the clusterfuck of thoughts crammed inside my head. I hate lying to Lila—hate lying to anyone —but if I'm ever going to end this—fight until the end— then I need to go through with the experimental amnesia treatment. Hopefully doing so will bring back enough of my memories that, at the very least, I'll be able to positively identify some of the people who took me and my siblings over four years ago.

I just hope remembering doesn't break me again.

*I won't let it pull me down.*

*I won't give in*

*To darkness.*

*Drown me all over again.*

*I'll fight and I'll fight and I'll fight*

*Against the rapids.*

*Against the terror.*

*I'll never surrender.*

After I finish jotting down my thoughts, I put the notebook in my nightstand. Writing usually calms me, but I still feel restless as hell. I need answers. It's driving me fucking crazy not knowing what's going to happen next—what the Soulless Mileas next move will be.

I sit down at my desk and turn on the computer screen. With a few clicks of the mouse, I open a webpage filled with information about the group. I scroll through the updated pages and read a more current post. Lately, there's been a lot of rambling about sacrifices. It makes me really damn anxious and worried that Sadie is their sacrifice—worried I could be too if they get their hands on me.

"The sacrifice isn't just about giving up what we want," I read a section of the article aloud. "It's about giving up what we love. It's the ultimate sacrifice and the aftermath will cleanse our souls."

A chill slithers up my spine. Was it my father who wrote this? Is that what we are to him? His sacrifice to cleanse his soul?

I shake my head, anger blasting through me. Fuck him. He doesn't love us, no matter what his twisted mind thinks.

No matter how much I want to be strong, though, the pain of what my father has done nearly kills me every time I think about it. The air is strangled from my lungs, making it difficult to breathe. I need to remain calm, stop stressing, and give myself a few hours to forget about all the shit going on in my life.

Only one other thing can calm me down when I'm this worked up. Or one person, anyway. Lyric Scott, my best friend, my girlfriend, my everything really. I don't even care if I sound cheesy. Lyric is the best thing that's ever happened to me, besides being adopted by the Gregorys.

After I slip on my boots, I go downstairs to the kitchen.

Lila is standing in front of the stove baking something that smells heavily of cinnamon, and Ethan is sitting at the table sorting through some papers for work.

"Can I go over to Lyric's for a while?" I ask as I grab a can of soda from the fridge.

Lila looks up from the pan, hesitation written all over her face as she exchanges a look with Ethan. "It's kind of late, don't you think?"

Ethan glances at the clock. "It's only nine."

Lila glares at him. Clearly, that's not what she wanted him to say.

I pop the tab on the can. "It's just next door, and there's an officer parked right outside… But if you don't want me to go, then I won't." The last thing I want is to stress her out.

Ethan shakes his head. "I don't think it's that big of a deal," he says to Lila. "And you can't keep him locked up forever. He's eighteen years old."

"Yeah, I know." She sighs, turning down the temperature of the burner. "I guess it's okay. Just make sure you make it home by midnight." She picks up a spoon and stirs whatever's in the pot. "Oh, and please keep Lyric's bedroom door open at all times."

"I will," I tell her, feeling slightly uncomfortable.

Ever since the Gregorys and the Scotts found out about mine and Lyric's relationship, they've been very adamant about an open-door policy. I'm okay with it, though, just as long as I get to see Lyric.

On my way out of the house, I pass by the living room. Fiona, Kale, and Everson are sitting on the couch, watching some sort of zombie movie on the flat screen.

"Where do you think you're going?" Fiona calls out when she spots me hurrying for the front door. At thirteen years old, she has a lot of spunk. In a way, she reminds me of Sadie, back before we were taken. Always playing around, always so excited about everything, and a bit over-dramatic at times. "Oh wait. I bet I know. You're going to see Lyric." She flutters her eyelashes, drapes her hand over her head, and flops back on the cushions. "Oh Lyric, I love you so much. I can't stand being away from you for more than ten seconds."

I shake my head, my lips quirking. "Lyric and I haven't seen each other all day."

"That might be a record," she says, sitting up on the couch. "Seriously, you guys have issues. When I start dating, I'm going to have a rule that we can only spend like two hours a week together."

Kale, who's almost sixteen, chokes on a laugh. "Yeah, I bet that'll never happen. With how dramatic you are, you'll end up being one of those girls who wants to spend every two seconds with her boyfriend."

"Hey, don't be rude just because you and Zoe broke up." She slumps back. "It's not my fault you got too clingy."

"I wasn't too clingy," Kale grumbles, pushing to his feet. "I just liked spending time with her." He squeezes by me and stomps up the stairs, slamming his bedroom door.

"Teenagers are so hormonal," Fiona says with an eye roll.

"You should cut him some slack," I say. "He's still really upset about the break up."

"He needs to get over it," Fiona replies. "He didn't even like Zoe that much."

"He might have." I lean against the doorway. "It seemed like he did to me."

"Yeah, well, he didn't," she says. "Trust me."

"Did you actually hear him say that?" I ask.

"Nope. I just know this stuff." She focuses on the television.

Fiona says these kinds of things frequently—that she just knows things she couldn't possibly just know. I once heard her tell her friend she believes she's a psychic, and while I'm not sure I believe in that kind of stuff, I can't help but wonder sometimes.

"Hey, you still coming to my game tomorrow?" Everson asks as I turn for the foyer.

He's fourteen years old and has been obsessed with football for as long as I can remember. His games are important to him and even though sports really aren't my thing, I want to go to his game, get out of the house, get some fresh air.

"I think I should be able to make it." I pat my pockets as I back toward the foyer again, making sure I have my phone on me, because I know Lila will text me a few times to make sure I'm okay.

"Cool." He stuffs a handful of popcorn into his mouth. "It might be the last one you ever get to see for a long time."

I pause. "How do you figure?"

He nonchalantly shrugs. "Because you're graduating and going on that band tour."

"I'm not going on the tour." Just thinking about my band, Alyric Bliss, going on the Rocking Summer Blast Tour makes my mood plummet. But I can't go with them. Not when the Soulless Mileas want me. Not when Sadie is out there waiting for me to save her.

"Yeah, right. You'll change your mind," Everson says. "I know you're going through some stuff and those crazy people are after you, but you like music almost as much as you like Lyric. And since she's going on this tour, you'll end up going."

I want to argue with him. Tell him he doesn't get it. That there's more to it than just some crazy people being after me. But a small part of me still hangs onto the hope that maybe over the next month my life will change, and somehow, I'll get to go on the tour. Lyric even insisted I go with the band to record next week. She said whether they replace me or not, I've earned the right to be on the album. My initial instinct was to argue, but I really want to be a part of this with them, so I agreed.

"I'll see you in a bit, okay?" I tell Everson then walk out the front door.

I make my way down the path to the driveway, the night summer air instantly making me sweat. As I'm rounding the fence to head next door, I spot a police car parked not too far down the road. The car is always there, watching my house, and when I go to school, therapy, or band practice, it tails me. I never get any time alone anymore, and I long for the days when I can walk down the sidewalk without being watched and without worrying that someone is going to grab me.

Live for the days when I can just *live*.

When I reach the side door of the Scotts' two-story home, I hear music blaring from upstairs, probably from Lyric's room. I rap on the door several times before I give up and just walk in. I don't cross paths with Mr. or Mrs. Scott as I make my way upstairs and to Lyric's room, something I'm thankful for, considering Mr. Scott seems uncomfortable every time I'm near his daughter. Lyric says it's because he's worried we're having sex. I want to tell everyone that they have nothing to worry about, that because of my fucked up past, I'm not sure when I'll be ready to have sex. I used to think I'd never get to a point in my life where I could even think about having sex. But when I met Lyric, some of that fear was overpowered by want.

*Want, want, want*
*All the time.*
*I want her so badly*
*I'm losing my mind.*
*With all the desire*
*And heat*
*Pulsating through me.*

I *feel like I'm stuck*
 *Out on a wire.*
 *Wanting to stay on*
*Yet wanting to fall.*
*Fall, fall, fall*
*Right into her.*
*God, please let me fall.*

I can't help but smile as I reach Lyric's bedroom. Her door is open, "Holocene" by Bon Iver is playing from the stereo, and she's sitting on her bed strumming her guitar and singing along with the song. Her long blonde hair flows over her bare shoulders, and she's wearing a pair of red shorts, a black tank top, and the leather bracelets we gave each other last Christmas. She's so beautiful that I have to catch my breath.

Instead of walking in, I linger in the doorway and

watch her play, getting lost in her singing. Lyric has an incredibly beautiful voice that gives our band an edge. I could probably listen to her sing all day long, if she'd let me. While she's okay with her stage fright, she gets nervous when people watch her sing, including me. She conquers the fright, though, every time she steps up on stage, which makes her that much more amazing.

As the song ends, she scrunches up her nose, clearly frustrated. She must be trying to work out something with the tune because the song turns right back on. She lines her finger to the guitar strings and her lips part, but she freezes when she notices me.

A smile spreads across her face, and her green eyes light up. "Hey, I was just thinking about you."

I don't know how she can look so happy to see me. She tells me all the time it's because I make her happy. That has to be a lie. Lyric is just an upbeat person. She smiles about ninety percent of the time, laughs the other nine percent of the time, and that one percent is for the rare occurrences when she's sad.

"Weird. I was just thinking about you too before I came over," I say with a small smile.

"That's because we can clearly read each other's minds." She sets down the guitar and stands to her feet, stretching out her arms and legs.

"If that's the case, then what am I thinking right now?" I ask as my eyes wander up and down her body.

"Hmmm…" She taps her finger against her lips with a sparkle in her eyes. "That you so want to kiss me right now."

My lips quirk in amusement. "How'd you guess?"

"Because it's always what you're thinking about," she

teases as she crosses the room toward me. "Morning, noon, and night, you can't get my kisses out of your head. Because they're that awesome."

"And apparently mind controlling," I joke, already feeling better.

"Well duh. Awesome kisses have to have the awesome power of mind control; otherwise, what'd make them awesome?" She grins, placing her hands on my shoulders.

"Maybe your kisses are just awesome because you're you," I suggest, tucking a strand of her hair behind her ear.

Her attitude shifts from playfully joking to intensely wanting. I know what she wants, so I dip my lips and give it to her. I kiss her softly at first, but the longer our tongues tangle the more I begin to tip sideways on that wire. I just want to let go. Tumble off and never get back on.

I back her up, kissing her passionately until our legs bump the side of the bed. We fall onto the mattress and she giggles against my lips. The sound makes me smile, but the light mood immediately heats up again as my hands travel up and down her sides, across her breasts and her waist. I kiss her with every ounce of emotion I have in me, but my body trembles as she parts her legs and grinds her hips against me. I fight the urge to stop, refuse to let the past control me.

*I won't go there anymore.*
*Back into the dark*
*Where I'm lost and all alone.*
*I won't let them control me anymore.*

"My parents aren't home," she whispers against my mouth as I slip my hand under her shirt.

I nod, even though she wasn't really asking me a question. Not straightforwardly anyway. I know her well enough to understand what she wants without her flat out asking for it.

I push back, grab the bottom of her shirt, and fumble to pull it over her head. Once it's off, I toss it onto the floor.

She stares up at me with her intensely green eyes as her fingers wander to the hem of my T-shirt. "Can I?" Her voice is soft as she carries my gaze.

I swallow hard then nod, wishing she didn't have to ask. Wishing I was strong enough to just get over my issues so I could be the kind of laidback, carefree guy she deserves. But it'll take time before I'll ever be able to jump off that wire without the inner fight rising inside me. I'm starting to believe that one day I'll get there, though, which is more than I could say a few months ago.

She sits up and I lean back so she can pull my shirt over my head. Then she tosses it onto the floor and splays her fingers across the tattoo on my side. She traces the lines of the feathers that form a phoenix, then her hands skate downward toward the top of my jeans. I shiver out of fear, out of want, my mind racing so quickly I barely register when she asks if this is okay. I dazedly nod and she skims her fingers back and forth across my lower abdomen, just below my waistband before she tugs on my belt loop, pulling me against her as she collapses onto the bed.

I stick my hands out to brace the fall, but she yanks on my jeans again until I lower my lips to hers. I kiss her slowly, taking my time, memorizing every inch of her mouth as my hands explore her body. The longer the kiss goes on, the more complicated it becomes to breathe, but in the best fucking way possible.

*I don't care if I die.*
*If I ever breathe again.*
*Just let this kiss go on forever.*
*Let it carry me away*
*To someplace better.*
*Where it's just Lyric and I*
*No past, only the future.*
*Let me be with her.*
*Let me get through this.*
*Let me get to a forever.*

I move back to remove her bra, then I crash my mouth to hers again as our chests collide. A shudder ripples through my body from the skin-to-skin contact. Fear resides inside me, underneath a sea of want, stirring.

*Don't forget.*
*Don't forget.*
*Don't forget.*
*What was done to you.*
*Don't forget that we own you.*
*Don't forget.*
*Don't forget.*
*Don't forget.*

I won't let it consume me. Won't let the past ruin this moment.

*No more. I'm stronger than this—than they are.*

Shoving the memory out of my mind, I focus on her lips, how incredibly soft they feel against my mouth, how her warmth engulfs me, and the pleading whimpers she makes as my hand wanders to the top of her shorts. My fingers linger there for a while as I fumble with the button. Once I get it undone, Lyric shimmies out of her shorts and kicks them onto the floor.

I take in her long legs, smooth skin, and beautiful green eyes. "I don't…" My fingers shake as I sketch a line up the inside of her thigh. "Are you sure you want me to touch you like—"

She pushes up and slams her lips against mine, answering my question. As we lie back down on the bed, my finger slips inside her, and I instantly become lost in everything that's Lyric. The way she lets me touch her. The way I'm the only one who gets to see her like this. The way she trusts me. How fucking gorgeous she is. How amazing her smile is. How amazing she is.

"Ayden." She moans my name as her eyes shut and she clutches onto my shoulders.

Good God, I'm about to lose it. Seriously. Somehow between the fear and uncertainty, desire has completely taken over. I don't even care that she's touching my shoulders, my chest, my stomach. All I can think about is getting to see her like this.

Once she comes apart, I brush her hair out of her eyes, place a tender kiss her lips, then roll on my side, letting my mind slow down.

"Are you okay?" she asks, rolling over and facing me.

I bob my head up and down. "I'm fine." When she still looks concerned, I take her hand and place it on my chest. My heart thrashes as my adrenaline soars. "I promise I'm okay." I swallow hard. "I love you and I trust you." To prove it to her, I move her hand down my chest, across my stomach, all over my scarred skin. It's tortuously confusing because I fear being touched yet at the same time, I want her to touch me more.

*Want. Fear. Want. Fear.*

*So closely tied together.*

*How can I untie them?*
*And make them come apart.*

"I love you too," she says.

Sometimes it feels so unreal when I'm with her, like I'm dreaming. Maybe I am. Maybe I'm really still stuck in that house and this is all just a dream, my mind's way of coping with what happened to me. If that's the case, then let me die in the dream, never wake up.

"No matter what you think, no matter how much you say you're not good enough for me, no matter what, I love you, Ayden," she says, as if she senses where my thoughts are heading.

Even though my body is quivering from her hands' exploration, my lips manage to turn upward. "That kind of sounds like the start of a song."

She leans over me, her hair veiling around my face. "What can I say? I guess you just inspire me."

"You inspire me too."

"We so sound like a cheesy love song right now." She grins as she sings, "You inspire me. I inspire you. Let's get together and run through a magical field of rainbows and butterflies."

I snort a laugh. "Don't pretend like you don't actually want to run through a magical field of rainbows and butterflies. I know how much you love them both."

"Okay, you might be right. But let's never, ever include rainbows and butterflies in our songs."

"*Our* songs?" I ask with a cock of my brow. "As in plural? Because we've only written one so far."

"You and I have a lot of songwriting in our future." As if she senses me tensing, she adds, "Ayden, I know you say you're not going on this tour, but I'm still holding onto the hope that you will." My lips part in protest, but she talks over me. "And even if you don't make it, I'll still be back in a few months, and we're going to pick up right where we left off. Nothing's going to change between us."

Reality seeps in and my body trembles even more.

Misreading my fear, she starts to withdraw her fingers, but I place my hand over hers, securing her palm against my chest.

"It's not that," I say in an uneven voice. "It just scares me... Thinking about being away from you for three months."

"It scares me too," she admits, giving in easily as I wrap an arm around her and pull her closer so our bodies are aligned perfectly.

Surprisingly, I stop shaking and a warm calm settles inside me. I give myself a moment to breathe in the inner peace, to let it really sink through me, because I don't get to experience calm very often.

"I know you think I'm being naively silly," Lyric whispers. "But I'm still hoping we won't have to be apart. That you'll go in on Monday and do this experimental therapy treatment, and the police will be able to find your sister."

I know that it's not going to be easy. That it may take several tries for the treatment to work. That if it does work, it might be like opening Pandora's Box, and my mind will be so fucked up that I'll be back to where I started before I came to the Gregorys'. There's also the possibility something could go wrong. That I could end up in shock, with more memory loss, or even heart failure. The risks are why Lila won't let me go, and why Lyric looks like she's going to throw up every time the treatment is mentioned.

"Hey, it's going to be okay," I tell her when I note the paleness of her skin.

"You don't know that for sure." She buries her face into my chest. "I don't want anything to happen to you."

"Nothing's going to happen to me." I smooth my hand over the back of her head, wanting to promise her I'll be okay no matter what happens.

But I can't bring myself to lie to her.

# Lyric

✿✿✿

I'm so worried about Ayden, my stomach hurts. My heart… God, my heart is having the most trouble. I'm not sure how to convince it everything will be fine, that keeping this secret for Ayden is the right thing to do. I want to tell someone so they'll stop him from going through with the treatment, but it feels selfish to do so. Not being able to help his sister has been silently killing him. If this treatment works—if he can remember enough to save his sister—then maybe he'll be able to finally, *finally* live his life in peace.

"You smell like vanilla cupcakes." My voice is muffled as I press my nose against his bare chest.

Ever since he told me he loved me, he's been getting better with being touched. But he still trembles sometimes, and when things get really hot and heavy, we have to stop before he veers toward a panic attack. Right now, he's extremely calm, though, at least for him, so I'm going to savor this moment for as long as he'll allow it to continue.

He tangles his fingers through my hair. "That's because

Fiona sprayed me with some girly perfume crap this morning. She used so much of it that it soaked through my shirt."

I laugh, nuzzling closer to him. "Really? Why'd she do that? Just to torture you?"

"She said I needed to sweeten up. That I was acting too grumpy and sour."

"Why were you acting grumpy?" I cross my fingers that he'll open up and tell me.

"I don't know… I think I'm just stressed and have been taking it out on everyone."

I inch to the side so I can set my palm on his chest and feel the rhythm of his heart. "Stressed out about the therapy?"

His heart slams against my palm. "I'm stressed out about a lot of things."

I angle my head back and look up at him. "But right now, you're worried about the therapy."

"Are you trying to play therapist?" he teases even though his pulse is still racing.

"Maybe." I push up, straddling him, and my pulse accelerates as his gaze drinks in my chest. "I just know how you are … that you shut down sometimes and don't talk about your feelings. What you're doing Monday is super huge, and I just want you to know that you can talk to me, and hopefully, I can help make you feel a little less nervous." I sweep my hair to the side and flash him a grin. "Making people feel better is one of my many talents."

"And just how are you planning on making me feel better?" he asks, grazing his fingers across my breasts.

Like every other time he touches me, butterflies lose their mind inside my stomach. "Well, I wasn't planning on doing *that*, but if that's what you want then…" I trail off as I lower my lips to his. "I'll give it to you."

A husky moan escapes his mouth as I suck on his bottom lip. He cups the back of my head and draws me closer, sliding his tongue into my mouth. My body doesn't feel like it's under my control anymore as I rock my hips against his. He groans, but stiffens. I know he wants to do this just as much as I do—I can feel his hardness through his jeans. But wanting and having are two different things with Ayden, and I wait for him to stop us, like he usually does.

But after counting under his breath, he kisses me more fiercely as he grinds his hips against mine. He repeats the movement over and over again, moaning and gripping onto my waist. My hips move rhythmically with his as I lose myself in him. My hands drift down his chest and to the top of his jeans. I want to touch him like he touches me.

*Touch him, touch him, all over.*

*Never let him go.*

I wait for him to stop me and when he doesn't, I undo the button of his jeans. His stomach muscles tense, but he continues kissing me. With a nervous breath, I dip my hands inside his boxers.

He groans something incoherent about trusting me as his body trembles. I worry I've pushed him too far, but then he seals his lips to mine and kisses me so forcefully I swear I'm going to have a bruise. I fall blindly into the moment, part of me wishing I never had to return. That I could just stay this way, him and I in this perfect place where he lets me touch him.

*If only I could hold on forever.*

*Hold onto him forever.*
*He's come too far*
*Just to fall all over again.*
I can't lose him.

The fear is always there in the back of my mind that therapy is going to change him, remind him why he has such a difficult time letting people touch him.

*What if I lose him?*

"You're not going to lose me," he breathes raggedly as he blinks up at me, his eyes glossy, like he's high from our kisses.

"Did I say that aloud?" I sound breathless. "Sorry, I thought I was talking to myself in my head."

He chuckles. "You know that makes you sound kind of crazy."

"Good for me you already love me," I tease. "Crazy or not, you're stuck with me now."

"That's perfectly okay with me," he says. "Just as long as... as long as you're okay with being stuck with me."

I don't answer with words. I answer with a kiss.

We make out for at least another hour before we put our clothes back on and lie down on my bed side by side.

"You should just spend the night," I say as I trace the folds of his fingers.

"I wish I could, but I don't think your dad would appreciate coming home to that."

"My dad's way more chill than he was when he first learned about us."

"Yeah, maybe... But since I want him to stay chill, I think I should probably not be in your bed when he gets home."

I jut out my lip, knowing he's a sucker for the move.

"That sounds like no fun at all."

He laughs, shaking his head as he rolls on his side. "As much as I love giving you your way, I can't this time."

"Oh fine." I sulk. "Can we at least do something fun tomorrow, though?" *Before Monday when everything could change.*

"I actually promised Everson I'd go to his football game with him." He strokes my cheekbone and my eyelashes flutter uncontrollably. "You should come with me."

"To a *football* game? Blah." I make a face. "But if that's what you're doing, then count me in." I dazzle him with a grin. "Man, it's a good thing I love you."

A small, rare smile graces his lips then he kisses me again.

"You taste minty," he whispers against my mouth. "And kind of sugary."

"That's because I just ate mint chocolate chip ice cream before you came over."

He takes another taste, before propping up onto his elbow. "Tell me something happy. I need happy right now."

"Happy, huh?" I drum my finger against my lips. "Well, today at school, I won an award for that project I entered in that art contest."

"Really?" The pain in his eyes briefly diminishes. "That's amazing, Lyric, seriously."

"Yeah, it's pretty cool. The sucky part is the award came with a scholarship, which I have no use for at the moment. My mom wasn't very happy about it, which I guess I get. I mean, she's an artist, and it's pretty baffling to her that she has a daughter who's turning down an art scholarship. I had to explain to her that while I love to draw, I'd much rather be singing and spreading my awesomeness through music, even if sometimes the thought of singing onstage makes me want to puke."

"Don't be so hard on yourself. You've been doing amazing with your stage fright."

"Yeah, I guess so." She mulls over something, seeming reluctant. "Can I ask you something?"

"You can ask me anything."

"What do you want to do?"

His fingers trail down my neck to my chest. "What do you mean?"

I roll on my side and hitch my leg over his hip. "I mean, when we graduate. Do you think you'll go to college ever?"

"Maybe … I actually haven't really thought about it too much."

"Well, now that you are thinking about it, can you see yourself tied down with classes?" I ask, eager to hear his answer.

"Not really." He contemplates his answer. "I honestly just want to play my guitar. It makes me feel calm inside and happy."

I smile at that. "I don't think you've ever said that before."

"Said what?"

"That something makes you happy."

"You make me happy too," he says softly.

"It's nice to hear you say that, Shy Boy. " I wink at him. "My life is now complete, which makes me very, very happy."

A ghost smile rises on his lips. "Good, I'm glad you're

happy."

"Of course I'm happy. I get to be here with you."

I expect him to argue that there's no way I could be happy with him, but surprisingly he doesn't.

*Progress.*

We spend the rest of the night talking and stealing kisses until midnight rolls around and he leaves to go home. I watch him through my window as he rounds the fence and heads up his driveway, only turning away when he's made it safely into the house.

Like everyone else, I constantly worry that at any moment those creepy people who are after Ayden are going to slink from the shadows and steal him away. Every night when I close my eyes, I dream of the days when I won't have to worry about losing him. That he'll be safe. That he'll be free of them.

Because I know those days will come.

I won't let myself believe anything else.

Sunday flies by quicker than I want it to, and before I know it, Monday arrives. Ayden's appointment is after school, and I'm severely distracted during classes, stressing over what's going to happen.

"Why are you acting all twitchy?" Sage, the drummer in my band, asks during math class.

"I'm not acting twitchy." I lie, unsure what to tell him since he doesn't know much about Ayden's situation.

He rakes his fingers through his blue hair, eyeballing the pen I'm tapping madly against the desk. "You aren't, huh?"

I cease the tapping and slump back in my seat. "There's just some stuff going on, and I'm having a hard time handling it."

He shoves up the sleeves of his grey shirt, revealing the multiple tattoos on his arms. "That doesn't sound like you. You always seem like you can handle anything."

"I try to, but I can't always be perfect." I flash him my pearly whites. "Everyone's got to have their flaws, and while mine are super small, I do have them."

"I wasn't saying you have to be perfect... I was just..." He studies me, fiddling with a piercing in his brow. "Is this about Ayden?"

Sage used to have a crush on me so whenever he mentions Ayden, things get a little weird and uncomfortable. But right now, I'm more concerned he might know what's been going on with Ayden. I have no idea how he'd know, but Ayden is a private person and would freak out if Sage or Nolan, the bassist of our band, found out.

"No." I glance at the clock. "Everything's fine with Ayden."

"Are you sure?" he questions, staring me down. "I know you've been struggling with him leaving the band... You've been distant at tryouts. It's got to be hard, trying to replace him."

"It's not about that." I chew on the end of my pen. "Well, it does kinda suck balls that we have to replace him, especially when everyone that's tried out sucks balls too."

"I think that might be the meanest thing I've ever heard you say." He seems amused by the fact.

"Why? I don't tell *them* they suck balls." I sigh when he keeps grinning at me. "Okay, I know I'm being a total Debbie downer right now, but seriously, how are we supposed to rock this tour if our guitarist can't carry a tune? We need to find someone spectacular. Or at least someone who can hit all the notes."

"Would you relax? We'll find someone," he reassures me, sitting back in the chair.

*I don't want to find someone. I want Ayden.*

The idea of being on the road, touring, is freaking amazing, and I know I'll go even if Ayden can't. But being away from him for that long is going to be torturous. Plus, the people who've tried out are in no way as musically talented as Ayden.

"But you might have to stop comparing everyone to Ayden," Sage says. "We might just have to settle for someone who's not as good as him."

"I know," I say, even though it kills me. It's time for me to start sucking it up and being the ever-so-amazing optimist I know I can be. "That one dude with the green hair might have potential."

He grins. "There's the Lyric I know."

"She's just a little tired." I pretend to take a bow. "But she decided she needed to quit hiding being her exhaustion and make a grand appearance.

We bust up laughing, but then the teacher forces us to quiet down.

A half an hour later, the final bell rings, dismissing school for another day. I hurry out of the classroom and zigzag through the packed hallway, making a beeline for Ayden's locker. I try not to freak out when he's not there. While he promised me I could go with him to the therapy appointment, I worry he'll pull a classic Ayden move and try to go without me, thinking he's protecting me somehow.

I bounce up and down on my toes, scanning the people lollygag through the halls, and then watch amusedly as Sage makes a U-turn when he spots my friend Maggie heading in his direction. The funny thing is, she does the same thing when she notices him. The two of them have acted so awkward since they almost hooked up. From what Maggie told me, they were both so wasted it ended up being a disaster, and they've barely been able to look each other in the eye ever since.

"What are you smiling about?" Ayden asks, appearing by my side out of nowhere, like a freaking ninja.

He's wearing a pair of black jeans and a grey shirt, and strands of his dark hair hang in his eyes that carry so much sadness. Although not as much as they used to.

"It's nothing," I say, shamelessly checking him out. "I was just laughing at Maggie and Sage and how they run away from each other every time they're about to cross paths."

He spins the combination and opens his locker. "I told you it'd never work out between them."

"Yeah, I know, but I kind of hoped it would." I slip my arm through the strap of my backpack and shrug when he shoots me a *really* look. "What can I say, I'm a dreamer." I sing the last part. "Who wants everyone to find love."

He laughs, but his expression conveys his nerves.

"How are you doing?" I recline against the locker beside his as I wait for him to put his books away. "I mean, are you nervous?" I shake my head. "Sorry, that's a really lame question, isn't it? Of course you're nervous."

"No question you ask is lame." He bumps the locker shut and slings his backpack over his shoulder. "I'm a little nervous, but at the same time, I'm kind of not ... It's

29

strange … I've been carrying so much pain and fear around with me ever since I came out of that house, but just the idea that maybe I'll finally put some of this behind me makes the pain and fear feel less heavy… If that makes any sense."

"It makes perfect sense." I lace our fingers as we make our way down the hallway toward the exit doors. "You're going to let me hold your hand while you do the treatment, right?"

"If Dr. Gardingdale will let you." He dazes off, and God knows where his thoughts are headed. Probably somewhere dark and filled with self-torture.

*I need to distract him.*

"My parents are going on a trip to Paris with my aunt and uncle," I say as we step outside into the sunlight. "They're going while I'm on tour, though, so I don't get to go."

"Sucks for them," he says, looking at me. "They're going to miss out on all the fun that would have come with bringing you."

I press my hand to my heart, giving him my best playful grin. "Hey, that's what I said too. But they just don't get it." I lower my hand to my side. "It's good, though, that my dad's spending time with his half-sister. And I have cousins now, so that's cool. There was just too much pressure being the only child in the entire extended family."

"Pressure?" he asks as we reach his car.

"Yeah, you know, to carry on the family name as awesomely as my rock star dad did. My grandma's said it to me a couple of times." I don't really feel *that* pressured. My parents and grandparents have always been cool about not pressuring me to be anything other than myself. I'm just trying to talk about anything other than the treatment and the tour.

"I'm sure you'll do fine." He opens the passenger door for me. "You're already going on a tour and you're only eighteen. That's a pretty amazing accomplishment." He smiles, but it's forced.

I know he wants to go on the tour. Wants to live a normal life. Well, as normal of a life as any other band member.

*Hurts, hurts, hurts,*
*All the time.*
*Watching him silently hurt.*
*The pain, the despair*
*He carries inside*
*It's got to be making him lose his mind.*
*Driving him to the edge*
*Of a place I can't let him go.*

"Yeah, I know." My mood goes kerplunk as I climb into the car.

*Only a few more hours and then it's time. Only a few more hours and I might lose him.*

Ayden suddenly freezes as he ducks to get in, and his gaze sweeps the grassy area across from the parking lot.

"Is everything okay?" I track his gaze to a woman wearing a red raincoat, standing in the midst of a sea of people dressed in summer attire. "Do you know her?"

He stares at her a beat longer, only looking away when the woman turns and gets swallowed up by the crowd. "Stay here." He closes the door and jogs back to the cop vehicle parked a few spaces behind us.

He says something to the officer before walking back to the car and climbing in.

"What was that about?" I ask as he shuts the door.

"I'm not sure, but the woman who chased me into the woods… She was wearing a red raincoat." He starts up the engine and locks the doors. "I don't think it was her, but I still thought I'd tell the officer."

My muscles ravel into knots as I skim the people around the quad and the parking lot. "What if it is her?"

"It's going to be okay." He places a shaky hand on my knee. "But we need to wait here until the officer comes back."

I gulp. "How long do you think it'll take him to check everything out?"

He shrugs, looking out the window. "That all depends on if he can find the woman or not." His jaw tightens as he shakes his head in dismay. "Lyric, I'm so sorry for putting you through this."

"Don't start," I warn. "You're not putting me through anything. It's not your fault those people are insane and won't leave you alone."

"It's kind of my fault, though, if it's my father who's in charge of their group," he utters quietly.

I reach over and set a hand on his scruffy cheek. "None of this is your fault. Trust me. Kids aren't responsible for the bad stuff our parents do. If that were the case, then I'd be responsible for every time my mom gets a speeding ticket when she decides she's going to race some dude in a sports car. Or when my dad secretly smokes in his office."

"Smoking and speeding tickets aren't really the same as kidnapping and murder."

"Ay." My heart is breaking for him. "You're the sweetest guy I've ever met in my entire life. You'd do anything for the people you love, so trust me when I say you're in no way responsible for anything that your father does. You need to stop being so hard on yourself."

He blows out a breath. "Maybe you're right."

"Of course I'm right." And a little shocked that I convinced him. "I'm always right, even when I'm wrong."

A half smile surfaces. "There you go again. Making up your own rules."

I open my mouth to keep going, but the officer knocks on the window, scaring the bejesus out of me. Ayden jumps too and quickly rolls down the window.

"It's all clear," the officer, who's probably in his mid-twenties, says as he leans down and looks inside the car.

"You found the woman in the red rain coat, then?" Ayden asks, still tense.

"I tracked her into the school," he says, nodding. "She's actually the art teacher, Miss Merrybellton, or something like that."

"And she was wearing a raincoat?" Ayden gapes at the officer in disbelief.

"I'm actually not surprised," I tell Ayden. "Miss Merrybellton can be a little," I circle my finger around my temple, "off her rocker sometimes. She's always trying all these new styles. Today must be inappropriate weather attire day."

"Well thanks for checking on it," Ayden says to the officer, his eyes still wide with fear and worry.

"That's what I'm here for. And it's good you told me. We need to check out all suspicious activity," the officer replies then steps back. "Now you should probably head home."

Ayden rolls up the window, pushes the shifter into reverse, and backs out of the parking space.

He's silent for most of the drive, which instantly puts me into worry mode. But every time I strike up a conversation, he gives me one or two word responses that lead to nowhere, and I worry he might be regressing.

My thoughts drift to my life before Ayden. I've always been a happy, positive person who's had a good life. My mom and dad have been the rock stars of parents, always showing me unconditional love. I've always been able to chase my dreams. I've always had a roof over my head. But even with everything, I still felt something was missing. That something was Ayden.

I didn't know it back then. Didn't realize it when we first met. It took me time to get there—took us both time. And now that I have it, there's no way I'm going to lose it.

When we get home, Ayden parks the car in front of the garage then twists in his seat to face me. "We have to leave in a half an hour." He chews on his bottom lip as he glances at the door of his house. "I'm not sure what to tell Lila since I normally don't go to appointments on Monday's."

"Just tell her you're stressed and need to talk to someone," I suggest, unbuckling my seatbelt.

"But how do I explain why you're coming with me? And why we're going to a doctor's office instead of the normal therapy office building."

My jaw just about smacks the floor. "We're going to a *doctor's* office?"

He slips the keys out of the ignition and opens the door. "It's just a precautionary measure in case something unexpected happens."

"I read a little about this treatment, and from what the articles said, you'll be put under sedation. Is that true?"

"I'll be under but I'll still be able to talk, at least from what I understand. But I think I'll be really out of it." When he sees the panic in my eyes, he cups my face between his hands. "Everything's going to be okay. Nothing's going to happen to me."

I swallow the lump wedged in my throat. The last thing he needs to be doing is worrying about me. I need to chill on the freaking out. "I'm okay. It's just a little scary thinking about what they're going to do to you."

He presses his lips together. "Are you sure you're okay? Because if it's too much for you, you don't have to go——"

I put a finger to his lips, shushing him. "I'm going with you. There's no way you're talking me out of it." I lower my hand to my lap. "And just tell Lila I need to spend as much time with you as I can before I leave for the tour."

"But what about the doctor's office thing?" He points over his shoulder at the cop car that's been tailing us since we left school. "Because they're going to follow us and report where we went the moment we park the damn car in front of the office."

I peek back at the cop car. "Are you sure you just can't tell Aunt Lila what we're doing?" Aunt Lila isn't really my aunt, just like Uncle Ethan really isn't my uncle. My family was just so close with the Gregorys from the moment I was born that I started calling them that.

"If I tell her then she'll never let me go through with it," he says with heavy remorse. "And I have to do this."

I try to bring out my sunshine and positivity as I rack my brain for a solution to our problem. "Just tell her you're taking me to a doctor's appointment. That I have to get a shot and need you to hold my hand."

"And what happens when she talks to your mom and finds out that was a lie?" he asks warily.

I shrug. "We'll face the music when it happens, but right now, let's just get through this one appointment."

"Are you sure you want to do this?" he double checks. "Because everyone's going to be pissed when they find out we lied."

"Of course I'm sure." I wink at him. "I got your back, dude. Always and forever."

That gets him to smile. I just cross my fingers that his smile will still exist after the therapy session.

An hour later, we're sitting in a waiting room at a busy doctor's office waiting for Dr. Gardingdale to arrive so we can get this show on the road. Ayden is about a million times more nervous than when he got his tattoo, which is saying a lot. But he's not the only one that's so jittery they can't sit still. It didn't help that when we left, Fiona blindsided me as I was getting into the car.

"I know what you're doing," she said with her hands on her hips.

I caught Ayden's gaze from over the roof of the car. "Look, Fiona," I turned to her and lowered my voice, "you can't tell anyone, okay? This is really important."

"I know it is. And I know I can't say anything to anyone, not when this could set Ayden free," she said simply. "I just wanted to give *you* a head's up that Ayden's going to need you to be calm for him. That it's important you don't freak out, even when things look bad."

For the second time today my jaw nearly hit the ground.

Her words have been stuck inside my head ever since, playing like a scratched record.

"What exactly did Fiona say to you in the driveway?" Ayden asks, leaning closer to me and keeping his voice low.

"It wasn't important." I pick up a pamphlet that's on the table to the side of me to busy myself with something since I can't seem to sit still.

"But she said she wasn't going to tell Lila and Ethan, right?'" A flush creeps up on his cheeks as his gaze drops to the pamphlet in my hand. Then he starts bouncing his knee up and down as he averts his gaze to the floor.

"No, she said she knew she couldn't tell anyone, whatever that means." I look down at the pamphlet to see what's causing him to blush. I try not to laugh, because out of all things, I grabbed one about safe sex. Seeing an opportunity to alleviate some of the tension, I decide to tease him a little. "It might have some good tips in there." I nudge his shoulder with mine. "Maybe we should read it."

He massages the back of his neck, muttering something under his breath before elevating his gaze to me. "You think we should?" The blush is still there, but his voice is surprisingly steady.

His unexpected question catches me off guard and I feel my own cheeks warm, which rarely happens. Usually I have mad skills in the chillax department, but just thinking about having sex with Ayden makes my heart go all glowy crazy in my chest like a cracked-out unicorn.

"I don't know." I fiddle with the edge of the pamphlet. "Maybe. The other night things did get a little …" I rack my brain for the right word that will sum up what happened Saturday night, but then decide to be funny, because we need funny right now. "Bow chicka bow wow."

He snorts a laugh. "I guess that's one way to put it."

"You're okay with what happened, right? I mean, I know that was a huge step for you." I fold and unfold the pamphlet, feeling super fidgety. "I just don't ever want to push you into doing stuff."

"Lyric, I swear to God I'm fine." His expression grows intense, his gaze boring into me. "You've never, ever have pushed me into doing anything that I didn't want to do." He blows out a frustrated exhale. "You've always been so patient with me, even when you shouldn't have to be."

I slip my fingers through his. "Ayden, I love you. Being with you is amazing. It's not about *having* to do stuff. It's about *wanting* to."

He nods his head up and down, his gaze dropping to the pamphlet in my free hand. "Still, it's getting easier… I mean, with the intimate stuff."

I lock eyes with him. "How much easier?" My voice is steady, but my heart's an erratic mess.

He opens his mouth to answer, and dear God, I'm eager to hear what's about to leave those lips of his, but an older dude wearing a bright-ass orange tie and tan slacks enters the waiting room, and Ayden instantly jumps to his feet.

"You haven't been waiting too long, have you?" Dr. Gardingdale asks Ayden, tucking his briefcase underneath his arm.

Ayden shakes his head. "Not too long."

"Good. Good." Dr. Gardingdale seems nervous, his gaze flicking back and forth between Ayden and me. "It's nice to see you again, Lyric."

Ayden reaches back, grabs my hand, and pulls me to his feet. "I hope you don't mind that I brought her."

"It's fine," he says, waving at us to follow him as he heads toward the door near the front desk. "Ayden talks very highly of you, Lyric. And it might be good that you're here. You seem to have a calming effect on him."

My gaze slides to Ayden. "Do you talk about me with him?" I'm not offended. Just curious what he could possibly have to say about me while he's in therapy.

He lifts his shoulders and shrugs. "You're a huge part of my life. Of course I talk about you." He holds the door open for me, looking a little sheepish. "Besides, like he said, you have this crazy calming effect on me, so whenever I get too stressed, I just start talking about you."

That makes me smile. I stand on my tiptoes, give him a quick kiss, then tuck the pamphlet into the back pocket of my shorts. He totally notices and his cheeks flush a deep red.

"You're so adorable when you're embarrassed," I say, taking his hand as we follow Dr. Gardingdale down the hallway lined with rooms.

"I'm glad you think so," he replies, his cheeks still pink. "Because I find it really fucking annoying."

I kiss his cheek just because I can.

When we reach a room at the end of the hallway, Dr. Gardingdale motions us inside, then closes the door. It looks like a normal check-up room; plain white walls that surround a bed, a blood pressure machine, and a couple of chairs.

"We're going to hook you up to the monitors so we can keep track of your heart rate while you're out," Dr. Gardingdale explains as Ayden sits down on the bed. "Dr.

Milleperton is also going to be putting in an IV as well so we can inject the sedative."

"An IV?" I ask in shock. "Is that really necessary?"

"This is an extreme treatment that requires some mild medication," Dr. Gardingdale says as he sets his briefcase on the counter near the sink. Then he turns to Ayden. "Now, are you positive you want to do this?" he asks. "Because there's still time to change your mind."

Ayden lies down, resting his arms on his stomach. "I'm not going to change my mind."

My heart speeds up, thrashing in my chest.

*Tell me what I'm supposed to do*
*To make this ache go away.*
*A gnawing warning in my heart,*
*Begging me to listen.*
*Soft whispers through my mind.*
*Tell me a story of where this is heading.*
*Tell me a story of my life without him.*
*Dark colors, no light, pure emptiness,*
*That's what the whispers promise me.*
*I've never been so confused,*
*So lost before.*

When the doctor comes in and hooks the IV and heart monitor to Ayden, I consider texting Aunt Lila. Consider running out of the room and bailing on the situation because I'm freaking out. But this isn't about me. This isn't about how I feel. This is about Ayden.

So, I take his hand, trying to be there for him the only way I can. "I love you," I whisper. "So much."

"I love you... too..." He trails off as he slips into unconsciousness.

# Ayden

✥✥✥

"Try to keep your mind clear," Dr. Gardingdale says as my hazy mind bounces back and forth between consciousness and unconsciousness.

"I'll… try…" My lips feel so numb, like they're detached from my face. In fact, my entire body feels like it doesn't exist.

"Good. Now try to picture the house you were kept in, if you can." Dr. Gardingdale's voice sounds like it comes from somewhere nearby, but I can't tell where he is—where anyone is. "But I don't want you to push yourself too hard, Ayden. If at any moment you feel like this is too much, just let me know."

"Okay…"

*Where's Lyric?* I want to say. *I want to see her. Want to make sure she's okay. She looked so worried the last time I saw her.*

But I can't see a damn thing. Can't feel anything. I just exist in an ocean of darkness threatening to pull me under the violent waves. I try to fight, try to keep above water, but eventually I succumb and have no choice but to go…

Down…
Down…
Down…

*Images flash through my mind, memories long forgotten of my brother, my sister, and myself. We're playing at the park, stealing candy from the gas station, painting the rocks in our yard to look like a rainbow, racing through the grassy field to the side of our home.*

*Then the memories shift away from my home life. I see myself in school, hanging out with my friends, and the time I walked home with Lacey Marlleron, a girl I had a crush on when I was thirteen. I relive getting into trouble when I was caught shoplifting. I see myself fighting with my mom over wanting to see my father. Fighting with my brother when I stole his skateboard and broke it. Fighting with Sadie over the bowl of cereal.*

*I see it all…*

*A life lost…*

*I see the fall…*

*That leads me straight to where the darkness all began…*

*And I plummet straight into it …*

*"You want to see?" Someone whispers in my ear. "Maybe if you're lucky, I'll take the blindfold off and let you look at your new home."*

*I start to tell them no, that I don't want to see anything ever again, but I have duct tape over my mouth. I want to scream. Beg them to tell me where my sister and brother are. I try to move, wanting to run the fuck away from this place, but metal cuffs bind my hands, and I'm weak from dehydration and starvation.*

*"Don't fight the pain, Ayden." Fingernails pierce into my hands, and I feel a warm trail of blood trickle down my skin. "The pain is the easy part."*

*I scream through the tape and kick my feet.* Stop. Touching. Me.

I'm so sick of being touched. I never want to be touched again.

*But she puts her hands on me again, letting them wander, before she removes the blindfold from my eyes and rips the tape off my mouth. "Open your eyes and meet your home."*

I shake my head. No. I won't do it. Won't do what she tells me.

*She stabs her nails into my hands again, this time deeper. Searing pain shoots up my arms and rips through my body, and I bite down on my tongue until I taste blood.*

*"Open your eyes," she warns, digging her nails even deeper.*

*I feel pathetically weak as I give into her request and open my eyes.*

*It's the first time I've seen the light of day in who knows how long. But with the dark curtains hanging over all the windows, hardly any light flows through the room covered in strange circular symbols. The carpet has stains on it, red stains that look like blood, and so much dust and dampness is in the air that it's hard to breathe.*

*"Hello, Ayden." A man is sitting in a chair in the middle of the room, and he smiles at me. "It's been a long time."*

What? Who the hell is this guy?

*"You're probably wondering who I am," he says, rolling up the sleeves of his stained shirt. "I was hoping you'd remember, but from the look on your face, I'm guessing that's not the case."*

*I eye him over, noting that he has the same eyes and hair color as me. A chill goes down my spine and my feeble body trembles.*

*"It's not really your fault. It's your mother's. She knew the deal when she had you—that she was supposed to raise you with the knowledge of who I am, then hand you over when it was time—but clearly, things didn't happen that way," he continues, snapping his fingers as he glances to my right. "Don't worry, though. I'm about to take care of it."*

*I turn my head to see what he's looking at and my gut churns.*

*"Please don't do this, Jerry," begs my mother as a woman with bright red hair and fingernails violently shoves her into the room. My mom trips over her gashed up bare feet and falls forward. With her hands bound, her face slams against the dirty carpet. Instead of getting up, she sobs, her body wrenching. "Please, don't do this. I'll do anything if you just let me go."*

*"No more bargains." The man rises to his feet and stalks toward her. "Your bargains aren't worth anything."*

*She lifts her head, tears streaming down her cheeks. "I gave you our children, didn't I? Just like I promised I would."*

*I forget how to breathe. How to think.* Our *children? That means ...*

*"Dad?" I gape at the man, horrified and disgusted.*

*He glances at me, and even though his eyes are like mine, they look unfamiliar, cold. Without saying anything, he grabs my mother by the arm, drags her to the chair, and pushes her down, then kneels in front of her.*

*"I know I gave you the children to take care of, but you haven't been raising them how we discussed. They know nothing about us or our beliefs." He exchanges a look with the red-haired woman, and she grins before rushing down the hallway. He focuses back on my mother, gripping onto her legs. "When I gave you the money to take care of them, I specifically remember stressing how important it was that you taught them about our way of life and about the sacrifice they'd be taking part in. But after talking to them, I see you haven't even told them who I am."*

*"I can give you the money back." A hysterical sob wrenches from my mother. "Just let me give you back the money."*

*"Give me the money back?" He cackles, a sound that sends an icy chill through my body. "We both know you spent that money on drugs a long, long time ago."*

*"I can borrow some from someone if you'll just let me go."* When he remains silent, she cries, *"Please, Jerry!"*

*"I have a better idea,"* he says as the woman with red hair returns to the room.

*"No... No... No..."* Tears pour out of my mother's eyes as the woman hands my dad a syringe.

*"What's the matter?"* He snatches hold of my mother's arm and twists her wrist. *"I thought this is what you wanted? That you'll do anything to get your hands this."*

*"Leave her alone!"* I shout, trying to wiggle my hands free from the cuffs. The metal bites against my wrists as I struggle and the scratches on my hand burn. But I keep fighting, refusing to sit here and watch him hurt her.

The woman in the corner snickers then sits down beside me. *"Don't worry. It'll be over soon."*

I'm not sure if she's talking about it being over for my mom or for me. It doesn't matter. I can't let either happen. I have to be strong.

*"Just let her go and I'll do whatever you want. Learn about you and your ways,"* I plead with my dad as tears stream down my face.

*"Oh, I know you will. But I can't have your mother messing that up for me. There was a lot of planning that went into bringing you, Sadie, and Felix into this world. You were supposed to be ready for the sacrifice. It wasn't supposed to be such a fight. You were supposed to be ready to cleanse your soul."* He looks at my mom then plunges the needle into her forearm.

I tell myself he just injected her with drugs. That she'll wake up like she always does whenever she shoots up. But as her body slumps to the floor, her skin turns sickly white. Her eyes open and veins map her rapidly paling skin.

A blood-curdling scream rips from my chest. *"No!"*

"Wake up, Ayden," someone says. "You need to wake up."

*I desperately try to open my eyes, try to blink the image of my dead mother away, but all I see is her lying on that bloodstained carpet where she took her last breath.*

"Open your eyes, Ayden … Please …"

*I'm trying. I'm really am.*

*Please, please let me get out of here.*

*Please don't let me die in this place.*

# Lyric

✿

I zone off as I hold Ayden's hand, recollecting every moment we spent together. It's funny, but when I really analyze our past, I can see that I fell in love with him way before I realized it.

That revelation puts a smile on my face. Then Ayden's body gives a hard jerk, and I'm yanked back to reality.

"Wake up, Ayden," Dr. Gardingdale says, rushing up to the side of the bed. "You need to wake up."

Ayden's body spasms and his eyelids start fluttering as if he's trying to wake up, but can't get his eyes open. Then the heart monitor starts beeping and panic skyrockets through my body as my worst fears are right in front of me.

"Open your eyes, Ayden … Please …" I beg, gripping onto his hand.

*Please don't let me lose him.*
*Don't take him away from me.*
*Just let me close my eyes*
*And pretend this is all a dream.*

Dr. Gardingdale tells me to move out of the way, and I

sink down in the chair. I've read information about this treatment, and my mind races with all the horrible things that could potentially happen. He could go into shock. Suffer from heart failure. Or worse, completely lose his memory,

*What if he forgets everything?*

Everything is moving in fast motion as the doctor starts talking medical talk while he injects something into Ayden's IV. I try to stay calm like Fiona said, but then the word "coma" comes out of the doctor's mouth and something inside me shatters. Tears stream out of my eyes as I slip out of the room to call Aunt Lila, knowing it's the right thing to do.

"Wait, Lyric, slow down," she says as I sputter out what happened. "I can't understand what you're saying."

I take a few measured breaths, trying to pull myself together. "A-Ayden did the treatment—the one you d-didn't want him to do. We're at a doctor's office down on First and Peach Way Lane. You need to get down here."

"He did *what?*" she exclaims. "Lyric, please, tell me he's okay."

"Just get down here, okay?" I tell her as the door behind me opens. Dr. Gardingdale steps out and motions for me to come back in. My chest tightens and air is ripped from my lungs. "Is he okay?" I ask him.

He nods. "You can come back in if you want to."

"Lyric, put Dr. Gardingdale on the phone," she demands before I hang up.

"Okay." My fingers tremble as I hand the phone to Dr. Gardingdale. "Ayden's mom wants to talk to you."

Sighing, he takes the phone and starts reassuring Aunt Lila that Ayden's all right.

I squeeze by him, rush into the room, and relief washes over me. "You're awake." Tears pour out of my eyes at the sight of him sitting on the bed as the doctor checks his heart rate.

Ayden's bloodshot eyes widen at the sight of my tears. "Lyric, I swear I'm fine." He opens his arms, indicating for me to come to him. "Please, stop crying. I hate seeing you cry."

Against the doctor's protests, I climb into the bed beside Ayden and rest my head on his chest, listening to his heartbeat. "I'm not going anywhere unless I have to," I tell the doctor. "So you might as well continue checking him."

The doctor sighs. "Fine. Just take it easy on him until I can check all of his vitals."

I nod and press my body closer to Ayden, breathing in his scent and warmth. "I thought you weren't going to wake up."

He rubs his hand up and down my back, tracing the length of my spine. "For a moment, I thought the same thing too." His voice cracks and he clears his throat. "But I'm okay now. Everything's okay."

I push to my elbows and peer up at him, trying to read his vibe. "Did it… Did it work?"

His gaze welds with mine as he nods. "I saw the house… I saw them."

I suck in a sharp breath. "You saw the people who took you?"

He nods again. "I saw the woman who…" He blinks down at the scars on his hands then looks back at me. "And I saw my father… Saw him…" He swallows hard. "Kill my mom."

I stop breathing, and for the first time in my life, I'm

speechless. My poor, sweet Shy Boy. Why does he have to keep going through so much pain? He's already been through so much already.

He brushes my hair out of my eyes. "I'm okay. I don't want you to worry about me … Everything's going to be okay now." He traces his fingers across my jawline. "I just really want to go talk to the detective."

"Your mother can drive you down there just as soon as I make sure you're one hundred percent okay," Dr. Gardingdale says as he enters the room, shutting the door behind him.

"You called my mom?" Ayden's brows knit as he stares at Dr. Gardingdale. "Why?"

"Actually, that was me." I pull a guilty face as Dr. Gardingdale hands me back my phone. "Sorry, I panicked."

"It's fine… I needed to call her anyway, considering what happened." Ayden sighs exhaustedly, his head slumping back against the bed. "I just don't like that she's probably worried as hell right now. I hate worrying her."

"I know you do, but trust me, we love that we get to worry about you." I sit up and press my lips to his.

*I'll kiss him over and over again*
*Every second I get a chance*
*After what happened*
*How can I not?*
*How can I ever not be with him?*

"Are you okay?" Ayden checks as he studies my face closely. "You look pale."

"I am now," I say, sitting down beside him. "You might have a real problem though."

His head angles to the side as his face contorts in confusion. "And what's that?"

"That you're never going to get rid of me." I thread our fingers together. "I'll never want to leave your side again after what just happened."

He chuckles, the tension momentarily vanishing from his eyes. "I'm perfectly okay with that problem. In fact, I think I should never, ever get rid of it."

"Good, because it's not going anywhere." I rest my head against his shoulder and close my eyes, breathing in the moment.

It's such a small thing, being here with him, but it feels so immensely important, because he's still him.

I just hope to God he stays that way.

# Ayden

E ven though it might sound insane, I thought I was
going to be stuck in that memory forever. Then I
heard Lyric's voice, pulling me back to her. When
I opened my eyes, there she was, leaning over me with
worry in her eyes.

Thankfully, the longer I grasp onto her the more she
settles down. If I could, I'd stay this way forever. But I
know I need to get to the police station so I can tell Detective Rannali about my father and give him descriptions
and a name.

*My father.* I involuntarily shudder at the thought of what
he did to my mother. All this time I thought she died of a
drug overdose, that she did it to herself. But my father
killed her, just like he probably killed my brother. What
really gets to me, though, is that the entire fucking thing
was planned. That my mother had us so she could give us
to these horrible people. That my father actually believed I
was supposed to be ready to take on his whacked out
beliefs.

I suddenly feel less guilty about what happened and really, really fucking angry. It's hard to sort through all my emotions when I'm so fucking torn.

*Hate or not.*
*Guilt or fault.*
*Live or rot.*
*I don't know what to do.*
*What kind of person I am.*
*Who to blame.*
*Myself?*
*My mother?*
*My father?*

Suddenly, the door bursts open and Lila barges inside with Ethan right behind her. Her anxiety is written all over her face, her eyes are wide, and her hair's a mess like she ran in a windstorm to get here.

"Ayden Gregory," she starts as she storms toward my bedside. A scowl etches her face as her lips part, but then she whispers, "I'm so glad you're okay."

Lyric scoots out of the way as Lila throws her arms around me and hugs me so tightly I can barely breathe.

"Don't you ever scare me like that again," she says with a few tears dripping down her cheeks.

Ethan gives me a pat on the shoulder and a sympathetic look as Lila continues to strangle me with her death hug. I notice Ethan's eyes are a little red, like he was crying before he got here. It makes me feel like the world's biggest asshole, because Ethan hardly ever gets too emotional, so he had to be extremely worried.

"I'm sorry," I apologize to both of them. "I just needed to do this, and I knew you'd never let me."

"You're damn right we wouldn't have." Lila steps back

and motions at the monitors around the room. "Because I knew something like this would happen."

"But I'm fine." I sit up and wince as my muscles groan in pain.

"I don't care if you're fine." She wipes the tears from her eyes with the back of her hand then waves a finger at me. "You won't do this treatment again."

"I don't have to do it again." I swing my legs over the edge of the bed. "I know who's been after me and who has my sister. I know what they look like and know one of their names."

Lila's eyes pop wide as her hand falls to the side. "The treatment worked?"

"Well, I don't remember everything." And I don't want to. After what I saw, all that pain and ugliness, I think it might be better if what happened to me is left locked in that box in my head. As long as my mind will let things be that way. "But I remembered enough." I stand up and the blood rushes from my head. "I need to go talk to Detective Rannali."

Ethan steadies me by the shoulder as I teeter sideways. "Careful. The doctor said that your body went through a lot of stress today."

"Maybe we should wait until tomorrow to go to the police station," Lila says, eyeing me over as if I'm going to break at any moment. "After you've rested."

"I'll never be able to rest until I talk to him." I force myself to straighten my stance. "Please take me there. I need to go. Now."

She and Ethan trade a questioning look, and then Ethan shrugs. "He's probably right. He'll be able to relax more after he talks to the police. He's been waiting a long time for this."

Lila shakes her head, still furious and upset, "Fine. But we're going to make this as quick as possible. I want to get Ayden home."

*Home.* The word carries so much more meaning now.

I'm so damn grateful to have a safe place to call home.

After Lila is reassured again and again that my health is okay, Lila and Ethan drive me to the police station. I want Lyric to go with me, but after the whole lying ordeal, her parents told her she needed to go home. I worry she's in trouble, but she assured me that she could handle what her parents consider punishments.

At the police station, we're forced to sit in the waiting area while we wait for Detective Rannali to return from a case he's out working on. I can hardly sit still, just thinking about how this might be reaching an end. That maybe they can finally find Sadie. Make some arrests. Give my brother some justice.

"I wish he'd hurry up." Lila bounces her foot up and down as she scans the busy room. "I want to get Ayden home."

"I know, but you need to relax." Ethan places his hand on her knee to settle her down. "Try to stay calm for him, okay?"

"I'm fine," I say, picking at a hole in my jeans.

"Don't say that," she says, startling me. "I know you

can't be fine, not after what you must have…" She sucks in a breath as her eyes water up again. "After what you saw."

"It wasn't that bad," I lie with my head tipped down. I shut my eyes and take a deep breath as the images try to resurface. "I didn't see that much."

She wraps an arm around me. "That might be true, but I know seeing any of it has to be difficult."

She keeps trying to console me until Detective Rannali finally shows up. His blue shirt has a coffee stain on it, his silver tie is loose, and his hair is disheveled. "I came here as soon as I could." He seems eager as he nods his head at his office door. "Come inside please. I'd really like to hear what happened with the session today."

The three of us rise to our feet, file into his office, and take a seat in front of his desk. Once everyone is settled, he opens a folder that contains the information and details of the stuff that's been going on over the last couple of years.

"I didn't know you were going through with the session," he starts as he searches his desk drawer for a pen. "But I'm glad you did. And I'm glad it worked."

"Don't treat this situation like it's a good thing," Lila snaps, being protective of me like she usually is whenever we're talking to the detective. "He could've been seriously hurt."

The detective clicks the pen and presses the tip to a yellow notepad. "I understand that. I'm just glad this all worked out."

"I didn't remember everything," I chime in as Lila grows more irritated by the second. "But I did remember some of the faces and a name."

He jots down a few notes, nodding. "How about you recount the details to me, and then we'll start going through some photos of possible suspects. If we can't get anywhere with that, we'll start working on a composite sketch."

I shudder at the idea of seeing my dad or the woman with red hair again, even if it's just in photos. But I nod, knowing I have to do this. Knowing this could be the lead they need.

I hurry and give him an account of what I saw while I was under. When I get to the part about my father killing my mother, the room grows so quiet you can hear everyone's heavy breathing.

"Ayden, I don't even know what to say." The detective shows the slightest bit of compassion. "This must be so hard for you."

"Say you're going to find him." I curl my fingers inward, balling my hands into fists, battling back the tears burning in my eyes. "Say you'll find him before he tries to cleanse his soul with Sadie's life, or whatever the hell he has planned for her. Then when you find him, you'll make him pay for everything he's done."

"I'll do everything in my power to make that happen," he assures me.

"Did you know about this cleansing soul thing?" I ask, gripping the armrests. "Did you know he—that the Soulless Mileas wanted to sacrifice someone they loved because they believe it'll cleanse their souls?"

His prolonged silence answers my question.

"You knew, didn't you?" I shake my head, struggling to keep my cool. But I hate how much I've been lied to throughout this investigation, how much they've left me in the dark.

"Over the last couple of months, I've learned enough

about these people that I've had a hunch for a while what they're intentions have been," the detective says, setting his pen down on his desk.

"Do you think that could be why my brother was murdered?" My voice comes out off pitch, wavering, jam packed with the sadness and anger I'm carrying inside me. "Do you think he was one of my dad's sacrifices?"

"At first I wasn't sure, but over the last couple of weeks we've stumbled onto some evidence that opens that possibility," he explains. "But Ayden, that's about all the details I can give you right now about your brother's case."

"And what about Sadie?" My tone is clipped. But I don't give a shit. I'm so sick of him not telling me what's going on. "Is she going to be next?"

He doesn't answer, instead pushing to his feet. "I'm going to need some more information from you, but I'd like to get you started on looking through some photos."

Lila turns to me, her skin pale. She seemed like she was going to faint when I told everyone my mother had us for these people and their sacrifice. I'll admit, telling that part hurt worse than nail scratches, broken bones, and wounded souls.

"Ayden, I can't believe… I don't know what to…" She struggles for words. "Sweetie, I'm so sorry."

"You don't need to say sorry. This isn't your fault." My voice is strained. "What's done is done and I just want to forget about it and move on. But after I help find my sister."

She nods, covering her hand over mine. "You can move on from this. In fact, I promise you that you will."

"I hope so." God, I hope so. Hope my sister's alive.

Hope that through all the darkness, there will be a light at the end of the tunnel.

I'm fucking restless as I get situated in front of the computer to scroll through photos. Blood roars in my eardrums as I wrap my fingers around the mouse. Lila is just as anxious, pacing the floor behind me while Ethan tries to get her to relax.

"Honey, you need to calm down," he says, wrapping an arm around her and steering her toward a chair.

"I'm trying." She bites her nails, looking at me. "Do you need anything? Water? A snack."

I'm not hungry but clearly she wants to help me. "Water sounds good."

Nodding, she springs to her feet and hurries off toward the vending machines just outside the room.

Ethan slumps back in the chair, letting his head rest against the wall. "I love that woman to death, but she doesn't handle stress very well," he mutters.

"I'm sorry," I say, knowing it's my fault. "For putting you guys through this."

"Stop apologizing, Ayden." He raises his head to look at me. "We're glad we get to be here for you. We just want you to be safe."

Nodding, I focus back to the computer. One photo after another, I sort through so many they all start to blur together. I'm there for so long that I worry maybe I won't find them.

But then my heart slams to a stop.

"That's him." I point at the photo on the screen of a man with the same eyes and hair color as mine.

"Are you sure?" the detective asks, leaning over my shoulder to look at the screen.

He looks younger in the picture, but I can still tell it's him. "Yes, I'm positive." My heart goes from a complete standstill to beating uncontrollably. "That's the man who killed my mother. That's my father."

*See his face.*
*It's branded in my mind*
*Like the tattoo on my side*
*Put there to remember.*
*You never wanted me to forget.*
*Guess what. I didn't.*

# Lyric

❦

I t's been a couple of days since Ayden did the treatment. For the most part, everything's been quiet in our lives. There hasn't been much drama, and we weren't even grounded for sneaking off to the therapy session. But Ayden is getting restless, waiting for something to happen with the case, although he won't say much about it.

I spend a lot of time trying to cheer him up, and from the outside it seems like it's working. But in the back of my mind, I worry he might not be dealing with stuff. It has to be hard for him. After finding out all those things about his parents. After seeing what they did. Finding out that his father paid his mother to have him.

My heart breaks for him and the pain he has to be going through.

"Did you hear anything I just said?" my friend, Maggie, asks me.

We're sitting in front of the school beneath the tree, lounging in the sun. We're supposed to be in class, but since it's the final day of school, and then I'll officially be a high school graduate, my English teacher let us have a free period.

"Not really," I answer truthfully, stretching my legs across the grass. "Sorry, I'm just a little distracted."

"You're always a little distracted." She rolls up her shirt to the bottom of her bra so the sun hits her stomach. "And I think I know why."

"Really?" I ask with skepticism. *There's no way she could possibly know.*

"Yep. It has something to do with a certain sexy Goth boy you can't keep your hands off of." She rests back on her hands, smiling smugly.

I relax against the tree behind me. "Okay, enlighten me then. Because I have no clue what you're talking about."

"Oh, you so do." She pulls her glasses down, looking at me from over the top of them. "I can see it in your eyes every time the two of you are within a mile of each other."

"See what?" I say innocently, only so she'll have to say it aloud.

"You know what I'm talking about." She sits up and tucks her legs under her. "But if you want me to say it then I will. I'm talking about S.E.X. *Sex.*" She raises her voice loud enough that the people around us can hear her. "You want to have *sex* with Ayden. You want him to put his—"

"All right. All right." I cut her off, laughing. "I get it."

"But do you really get it?" she asks, retrieving a tube of lip-gloss from her purse.

"Maggie, I love you to death, but I'm totally not following you."

She applies a coat of gloss then smacks her lips

62

together. "I'm asking you if you get how much the two of you need to get your freak on."

"Okay, we've talked about that reference," I say. "No calling it getting our freak on. It makes it sound so gross."

"Sometimes, it is gross." Her nose scrunches. "Like with Sage."

"Don't go there." I point a finger at her. "If you tell me things, I might not be able to look him in the eye anymore. I need to be able to do that for the sake of the band."

"Fine." Her eyes sparkle mischievously as she sits back in the grass. "I won't tell you all the horrible details just as long as you admit you want to have sex with Ayden." When my lips remain sealed, she adds, "If you want, you can call it making love, but I kind of wish you wouldn't." She pulls a face like the idea is appalling.

"Fine, I'll admit it, just as long as you'll drop the subject of my sex life."

She grins, bouncing up and down. "So you're saying it's true? You're thinking about having sex with Ayden?"

I nod, trying not to smile idiotically. But the idea of being with Ayden like that makes me grin. "I think about it a lot."

"Think about what a lot?" Ayden asks from right behind me.

Maggie smirks at me then bats her eyelashes as she looks up at Ayden. "About you and her getting your freak on."

I glance over my shoulder at Ayden and offer him an apologetic look. "Just ignore her. She ate too much lip gloss today."

"Hey, I don't eat it," she protests. "I use it to draw attention to these bad boys." She smacks her lips.

Ayden's never been a fan of Maggie, and he simply stares at her before focusing on me. "Why aren't you in class?"

I shrug, picking at the grass. "We got a free period so we thought we'd come chill in the sun. What about you?" I look at the parking lot behind us where I think he just came from. "Did you just get back from somewhere?"

"Yeah, I did." His gaze flickers in Maggie's direction.

I get to my feet, reading his mind, because we're in sync like that. "Hey Mags, I'm going to go talk with Ayden for a bit. Catch you later, okay?"

"Oh whatever." She stands up, brushing the grass of her legs. "I know you two are going to go make out in the car." She winks at me before strutting across the grass, giving her ass an extra shake as she walks by a group of football players.

"We need to talk, huh?" Ayden asks, his brow cocking.

"I could tell that you wanted to." I gently tap the side of his head. "Remember, I can read everything going on in there."

A soft laugh escapes his lips, but he quickly turns serious. "I do want to talk, actually." He gives a quick scan of the campus yard. "But maybe somewhere where there aren't so many people around."

The air is stifling today and I'm roasting like a beast, even in my purple tank, denim shorts, and gladiator sandals. "I am in desperate need of some air conditioning." I loop my arm through his. "How about we go sit in your car?"

He nods and we start across the grass, the sunlight flickering between the tree branches canopying above our heads. Neither of us speaks as we cross the parking lot and get into his car. I can tell something's stressing him out, and that he's stuck in his own little Ayden world of despair. I don't push him to confide in me, though, figuring he's been pushed too much already. If he wants to talk, then we'll talk. If he wants to sit in the car with me and simply hold my hand, then that's what I'll do.

He turns on the engine to crank up the air, then sits back and cracks his knuckles while gazing out the window.

"I'm sorry Maggie's a perv," I say as I prop my feet against the dash.

He glances at me from the corner of his eye. "I'm used to Maggie and her mouth. In fact, my day would seem oddly incomplete without hearing at least one dirty remark from her."

"Well, that's a huge change for you. Usually, you get irritated when she opens her mouth."

"I said I was used to her, not that I wanted to be used to her." He's smiling and it's so beautiful and rare that I have to grin along with him.

"I think I might be with you on that," I say. "Can you believe she tried to tell me everything that happened between Sage and her? And I'm talking *everything*. Could you imagine? I'd be scarred for life."

"Sage would be so pissed if she did." He rests his head back and stares at me for a heartbeat or two, his eyes smoldering so intensely I have to catch my breath.

*I never thought it could be like this.*
*That love could be so raw and potent.*
*So intoxicated.*
*So mind erasing.*
*My breathing is fading.*
*My heart isn't cooperating.*

JESSICA SORENSEN

*Anymore.*

"I found out something … about the case," Ayden says with a heavy sigh. "Lila actually pulled me out of class to tell me. Then she made me go talk to Dr. Gardingdale to make sure I was handling everything okay."

I practically get whiplash going from joking about Sage and Maggie's dirty rendezvous to talking about the case.

"What happened?" I sit up straight, my feet falling to the floor. "Did they find them? Did they find your sister?"

He reaches forward and gently places his hand on my arm. "Lyric, calm down. Nothing has happened yet. They just got a lead."

"But that's good news, right?" *Please, please, let it be good news.*

"I'm not sure." He seems so calm, which is strange. "Maybe. The detective said he'd give me an update when he had one. It might take a few days, though."

"Are you sure everything's okay?" I ask him for the eleventh-hundred time since the amnesia session. "You've seemed sort of, I don't know, sedated lately."

"That's not a bad thing," he assures me with a forced smile. "It's good to be calm, right?"

I nod, but I'm not buying it. I have a hunch Ayden's cool-as-cookie-dough-ice-cream behavior is like a calm before the storm. I want to press him to talk, but worry I'll only stress him out more.

*What do I do?*
*To get through to you?*
*To get inside your head?*
*See your thoughts.*
*Feel what lies under your skin.*
*In your veins.*

66

*In your heart.*

The bell rings and I sigh as we get out of the car to go to class.

"If you get a free period, meet me out front, okay?" Ayden asks as we part ways in the hall.

"Surely durely." I throw him a wave over my shoulder, then make a quick pit stop at my locker to douse myself in perfume because I'm one sweat away from having a serious case of BO. As I click open my locker, a piece of paper floats out and lands on the floor by my feet. Not thinking too much of it, I bend down to pick it up and realize it's a letter.

*We found the way to Ayden's heart. Make sure to pass along the message.*

My attention whips up, and I cast a panicked glance up and down the hallway, skimming the faces of everyone. I swear I see a blur of red race out the front door, but I'm not about to chase the person down.

I grab my phone out of my pocket and run straight for Ayden.

# Ayden

❧

"Lyric, what's wrong?" I gape at her as she races up
to me in the hallway, her eyes wild with panic.
Panting, she hands me a piece of paper while
dialing someone's number on her phone. "This was in my
locker." She hunches over, bracing her hands on her knees
as she catches her breath.

My hands shake as I read the note. *"We found the way to
Ayden's heart. Make sure to pass along the message."* More fear
than I've ever felt pulsates through me. They left this in
Lyric's locker. My Lyric. God fucking dammit! "Fuck." I
kick the locker, then grab Lyric's hand and guide her with
me as I stride down the hallway and burst out the exit
doors.

"Where are we going?" she asks as she jogs to keep up
with me.

My gaze is everywhere, taking in every person, every
door, every vehicle. "I'm getting the police." Getting her to
safety.

When I reach the police car, I startle the officer when I

rap my knuckles on the window.

He rolls the window down, his brows knitting. "Ayden, is everything all right?"

Shaking my head, I hand him the note. "This was in Lyric's locker."

He reads the letter and mutters, "This sounds like a threat." He curses then hops out of the car. "You two go wait in the main office while I check the area." He calls for backup as we jog across the yard, parting ways at the entrance door.

"Do you think they're still around?' Lyric asks as we hurry down the now empty hallway and toward the main office.

"I don't know." I keep ahold of her arm, never wanting to let her go. "I honestly don't think so."

Her eyes are wide as she works to keep up with me. "Why?"

"Because I think this is another way of them messing with my head," I say as I yank open the door to the main office. "This has to be part of their plan. Every one of their moves always seems so calculated. So deliberate."

The question that's really bothering me, though, is how did they know about Lyric? The answer is fucking terrifying. That they've been watching me close enough to know how much she means to me.

I don't know what their intentions are with putting the note in her locker, but I have a feeling the move was deliberate. Maybe they're going to try to use her to get to me. Or maybe they think they can scare me into handing over myself by threatening her. If that's the case, then they're right. I'd walk straight into their hands if it means she'll be safe.

# Lyric

❧❦❧

After I find the letter, I call my mom while Ayden and I wait in the main office. The police make a huge scene as they search the school. Thank God it's our last day; otherwise, we would've had to spend the rest of our school days with everyone gossiping about what happened. While I can handle staring, Ayden, my Shy Boy, has trouble with extra attention.

Aunt Lila is the one who ends up picking us up, because she's closest to the school. But my mom, my dad, and Uncle Ethan are headed home.

By the time Lila arrives, the police have searched every nook and cranny of the school and surrounding area and found no sign of who left the note.

She doesn't say a word as she barges into the office and strides straight for Ayden. "This has got to stop." She throws her arms around him, hugging him tightly. "They can't keep doing this to you."

"They didn't do it to me." Guilt laces Ayden's voice. "They went after Lyric."

Aunt Lila looks over Ayden's shoulder at me, then she snags hold of my arm and tugs me in for a hug too.

"I'm so glad school's over," Lila whispers as she continues to trap us in her death-grip-three-way hug. "Now we can keep an eye on you all the time."

"That's not completely true," Ayden says. "You have lives. You can't watch me all the time."

Aunt Lila is quiet, and I can almost see her wheels turning, trying to find a way to make it possible for her to be a near Ayden at all times. She must not arrive at a conclusion, because she says, "Let's get you two home, okay?"

We nod and follow her out to her car, leaving Ayden's vehicle there for Uncle Ethan and my dad to pick up.

Ayden barely utters a word the entire drive home, and I can see where this is heading. That he's blaming himself for the letter ending up in my locker.

"I know what you're thinking and it's not your fault," I hiss under my breath as Aunt Lila pulls the car into the driveway of the Gregorys' home. "So stop going there right now."

He turns his head away from the window, making eye contact with me for the first time in hours. "Lyric, they threatened *you*. I can't just forgive myself for that."

I scoot closer to him. "There's nothing to forgive. Nothing happened. I got a letter. So what. They didn't actually do anything to me. They just wanted me to pass along the message."

"You heard what the officer said," he whispers, self-torture rising in his eyes. "That letter was a threat."

I point at a cop car parked at the end of the driveway. "It's a good thing we have those then. Besides, they're always sending you threats and notes. This was probably just another way to try to get to you."

He crosses his arms. "I never should've dragged you into this mess."

"You didn't *drag* me into this mess. I willingly ran head on into it, and I'd do it again in a heartbeat just as long as I got to be with you." I cup his chin in my hand, forcing him to look at me. "Now, you're going to chill out, and we're going to go inside and work on our songs so we can kickass at the recording tomorrow."

"But I—"

"No buts," I scold, but also smile to shine positivity to all the darkness trying to rain down on us. "We're going to go practice, then we're going to make out after we're all finished."

From the front seat, Aunt Lila clears her throat. "I'm going to go inside and give you two a moment. Please, don't stay out here too long." She opens the door to climb out. "And Lyric, I want you to wait with us until your parents come home. They don't want you leaving for any reason."

I salute her and she shakes her head like *oh Lyric, you're such silly girl*. Then she ducks out and closes the door.

I fix my attention back on Ayden. "Now promise me that you'll stop blaming yourself for what happened."

"It doesn't matter if I can forgive myself," he says, looking at me with those sad puppy dog eyes of his. "Other people are going to blame me."

"You mean my parents?" I ask and he nods. I link my arms around the back of his neck and slant toward him until our chests are flush. "I'll tell you what. If they blame you then you can sink into your self-pity. But if they don't, you have to stop blaming yourself. And I mean it. No self-blame. No sinking into your pain. No torture and despair."

He considers what I said, his lips twitching as he restrains a smile. "You know, you're starting to sound like a walking lyrical book."

"It's probably because I've been writing, like, all the time. I want to come up with some fresh stuff that maybe *we* can use on the tour." I wait for him to argue about the *we*, and when he doesn't, I go back to our deal. "Now promise me you'll do it. Promise me you'll forgive yourself if my parents don't blame you." I lean back and stick out my pinkie.

He sighs, but hitches his pinkie with mine and seals the deal. "Fine, I promise."

"Good." I give my best prize winning grin because I know I've won the deal already, since my parents aren't the kind of people to ever blame Ayden for what happened. They like him more than Ayden thinks. They've always wanted me to be friends with him, even before we all met him.

I remember the day I was headed to meet Ayden for the first time. While I was walking over to the Gregorys' with my parents, I tried to get out of going, mainly because I was bored and wanted to do something fun. My dad said something to me that still gets to me when I really think about it.

"You're really lucky to have *every* single one of us," he said. "And you should really get to know the new kid. He's your age, and I'm sure he could use a friend with … Some of the stuff he's been through. You could be that friend for him. Do something good."

It's amazing how much I followed his advice. But being

friends with Ayden was never about doing something good. It always came so naturally, as if we were supposed to be friends long before we ever met. And if anything, he's the one who did something good for me, by letting me into his world. It's always made me feel so special that he's trusted me so much.

After we get out of the car, Ayden and I go into his house and up to his room to work on our song that we're supposed to be singing together on our album, but we spend a lot of time kissing too. About a half an hour later, the crazed parent mob shows up and we're summoned to the kitchen. They tell Fiona, Everson, and Kale to go into the living room and work on their homework. After the room is cleared of the youngin's, Ayden sits down at the table with Uncle Ethan while my worried mom sideswipes me with a hug.

"Oh my God, I'm so glad you're okay." She circles her arms around me, squeezing so tightly I feel like my lungs are being crushed.

I give her a moment before I step back. "I'm fine, Mom. Would you relax? Nothing happened."

"I will not relax, Lyric Scott. We were so worried." She has yellow, green, and red paint spots on her shorts and tee and even in her auburn hair, which means she probably rushed away from one of her art pieces.

I feel bad that she had to bail in the middle of a piece. As an artist myself, I know when inspiration strikes, you just roll with it until it stops; otherwise you could totally lose the vibe.

"But I'm fine." I span my hands to the side and curtsey, trying to lighten the stressful tone taking over the Gregorys' kitchen. "See, one hundred percent okay."

My mom shakes her head exhaustedly. "You know, I'd ask you how on earth you could possibly joke at a time like this, but I already know my answer." She shoots my dad a look.

He's sporting his infamous bedhead/fauxhawk hair, a style that's unintentional and only appears when he's really stressed and has been raking his fingers through his hair.

He pulls a *whoops* face then shrugs. "Sorry, but you knew what you were getting into long before you married me." He turns to me, his amusement vanishing as his arms fold around me. "I was so fucking worried about you," he whispers in my ear so only I can hear.

"I know," I whisper back. "But it's okay. It was just a note."

"Still, we're going to keep an extra eye on you," he promises. "No going out alone or anything."

I nod my head up and down. "That's fine by me, but Dad? This isn't Ayden's fault." I keep my voice low so no one else will hear me.

"Of course it's not," my dad says, sounding shocked. "Why would you say that?"

"Because he thinks it is."

We hug for a second longer then step back, forcing ourselves to relax for the sake of the others.

My dad walks over to Ayden, who's sitting in a chair at the table, staring at the floor, looking so sullen I want to cry for him. "You're okay, right?" he asks Ayden.

Ayden glances up, looking startled by my dad's question. "Um, yeah, of course." He looks at Aunt Lila, Uncle Ethan, and my mom who are all staring at him with concern.

He may blame himself for all of this, but there's

nothing but love for him right now. I just hope he can see it.

"Good. Good." My dad yanks his fingers through his hair, making the strands go even more askew. "If you guys want, we can move the recording to a later date."

"No way," I protest at the same time Aunt Lila says, "I think that's a good idea."

I scrunch my nose at her. "That is so not a good idea and it'll totally set us back for the tour."

She shoots me a warning look from across the kitchen. "Lyric, I don't think the tour is the most important thing right now."

"It might not be, but right now everyone is so stressed out it's starting to give me a headache," I say, stealing a sugar cookie from the plate on the counter. "No one laughs anymore. Tells stories. Smiles. It's all stress over this. Stress over that. And I really think everyone just needs to take a chill pill and focus on some fun stuff in life, even if it's just for a few hours. Then you can all go back to acting twitchy and crazy." The four of them give each other curious glances, so I keep on rolling. "What I think we need is for all of us get in the car and go do something fun."

"And what do you propose this fun thing should be?" my dad asks, mildly amused.

"I don't know." I give a shrug. "I didn't get that far when I was mentally preparing my speech."

My dad looks at my mom who glances at Aunt Lila. Obviously, she's the ringleader in their quartet.

"It might be good for everyone to get some fresh air," she finally says after seconds tick by. "Just as long as we go someplace safe."

"And relaxing," I add, stuffing the rest of the cookie into my mouth.

"Hmmm…" My dad rubs his jawline. "I might know just the place."

My dad is a kickass rock star/music producer, so when he said he knew a place that was both safe and relaxing, I was thinking maybe like a chill club that allows kids or perhaps a restaurant where the adults can drink a lot of wine. But nope. He takes us to Rock in Time Playhouse and Grub, which is pretty much a bedazzled pizzeria full of games, bouncy houses, and slides.

The second we step in, Fiona, Everson, and Kale race for the arcade section. Aunt Lila and Uncle Ethan chase after them while Ayden mutters something about needing to go to the bathroom.

"I'll be back in a sec," my mom says then wanders off to the bar to order a drink, leaving my dad and me to get a table and order food.

"You know we're all over twelve," I say to my dad as I point to the No Kids Over 12 sign beside the ball pit. "That so sucks. I want to jump in there like I used to do when I was a kid." Back when everything was so simple, so easy, so effortless.

He waves me off, heading for a corner booth. "That rule doesn't apply to us."

"How do you figure?" I ask as I weave passed the empty tables, following him.

"Because I know the guy who owns this place."

"Man, how many people do you know? Because it seems like a lot."

"It comes with the territory of running my own business." He slides into the booth and plucks a menu from a rack in the center of the table.

I plop down in the booth and cross my arms on the table. "I'm sure it might have something to do with the fact that you're a retired rock star."

"Perhaps." He fixes his attention on the menu.

"How do you do it?" I ask. "I mean, handle people giving you all these special favors and acting weird around you."

He shrugs, glancing up at me. "I'm not going to lie. Sometimes it's not easy and it gets tiring—it's part of the reason why I retired—but it was fun for a while."

"Do you think I'll be able to handle it? I mean, the environment." While I'm a pretty confident person, I value his opinion.

He rests his arms on the table as his mouth curves to a frown. "As much as I want to say no and keep you home with me forever, I honestly think you'll do just fine. You're an amazing girl and very level headed." He grins at me. "Plus, you've got my charming personality."

"That I do. You're going to let me go, though, right? I mean, you're not going to try to keep me home, like Lila's doing with Ayden."

He shakes his head. "Of course not. Besides, I think it'll be good for you to get away from here for a while and have some fun. Your senior year has been really stressful."

"I know." I spin a saltshaker in my hand. "I just wish Ayden was going with me."

"I know you do, but you have to understand how hard

it's got to be for him to even think about going when his sister still hasn't been found. Plus, I don't think anyone will be able to convince Lila to let him go."

"Yeah, I know." I sit back in the seat, trying not to let my disappointment get to me. While I'm bummed, I know Lila and Ethan have every right to worry about Ayden. And everyone's probably right. It's probably too dangerous for him to go. But the dreamer side of me can't help but think how much Ayden might regret missing out on this. He's missed out on so many life experiences already

*Missed.*

*Missed.*

*Missed.*

*I'm going to miss Ayden.*

*I'm going to miss everyone.*

"Dad, I'm really going to miss these talks of ours while I'm gone," I feel the overpowering need to tell him.

"I am too, Lyric." He chokes up. "But you know I'll always be here for you. Whenever you need to talk, just call me. In fact, I insist you call me at least once a day."

I stick out my pinkie. "Deal."

He hitches pinkies with me, offering me a small smile. "You know I'm the one who taught you how to promise this way, right?"

"I remember. I was four and you were promising me that you'd be home for my birthday even though you were on tour."

"You really remember that?" His eyes gleam with hope.

"Of course I remember. Just like I remember you never broke one single promise. You're an awesome dad. Always have been." I shoot him a cocky smirk. "That's why I turned out so awesome."

"You did turn out pretty freakin' awesome, if I do say so myself." He returns his attention to the menu, trying to discreetly wipe the tears from his eyes.

I really am going to miss him—miss everyone.

I glance at Kale and Everson freaking out over of a buttload of tickets pouring out of a machine, at Fiona and Ethan playing the arcades, and at my mom and Aunt Lila at the bar, sipping on wine, and laughing about something.

I smile to myself at how happy they all look.

*Mission of Fun accomplished.*

As I look back to my dad, I note all the tables around us are empty and a thought occurs to me. "Did you ask the owner if we could have this place to ourselves for the day?"

"I might have." He smiles as he reads over the menu.

"Nice job, daddy-o. I'm sure everyone will appreciate the down time."

But there's one thing missing from this picture of fun. Something I think I need to go check on.

"I'll be right back." I jump to my feet and wink at him. "Order me a beer while I'm gone."

My dad just shakes his head and mutters, "So much like me."

I wind past the tables and burst into the men's room.

Ayden is leaning against the tile wall with his head tipped back, his gaze locked on the ceiling. He jumps at my sudden appearance, his eyes popping wide. "Holy shit, you scared me."

"No more sulking," I warn, aiming a finger at him. "You promised me if no one blamed you that you'd let it go."

"I wasn't sulking," he tries to assure me. "I was just thinking."

"About what?"

"About…" He drags his fingers through his hair and puffs out a breath. "About us."

My expression fizzles to a frown. "It's never a good sign when someone is over analyzing their relationship."

"No, it's a good thing this time. I swear." He strides toward me, stopping only inches away, panic gleaming in his eyes. "I don't want to be a selfish person, but I can't stop myself from wanting to be with you. When I saw that letter… I realized how easily I could lose you and how much it'd kill me if it happened."

I thread my fingers through his. "Then don't lose me. Be with me."

"It's not that simple." He lets out a frustrated breath. "Every time something happens, I can't help but worry that something bad's going to happen to you and it'll be my fault."

"Nothing's going to happen to me," I press.

"You don't know that for sure," he mutters.

"Okay, you know what, I don't." I tug on his arm, pulling him closer to me. "But something bad could happen at any moment, even while we're standing here. Like the roof could cave in and crush me. That wouldn't be your fault, and you can't control it from not happening."

"Why would the roof cave in?" he questions with a trace of a ghost smile.

I give a half shrug. "I don't know, maybe that foul stench is rotting it away."

He chuckles but then his mood nosedives. "I get your point, but I don't think you're getting mine."

"Okay…" I study him closely. "Could you explain it to

me then, because apparently, my mind-reading skills are a
little wonky right now."

"You were right about what you said … That no one
smiles anymore. Not even you."

"I smile." I grin just to prove my point.

"But not as much as you used to."

"Ayden, that's not your fault—"

He places his finger to my lips, shushing me. "I'm not
saying it's my fault. I'm just saying that you deserve to
smile more, which I know you will when you're on the tour.
In fact, I bet you'll smile so much you'll even get Sage to
join in." He lowers his hand, tracing his fingers down my
chin, to my neck, and the collar of my shirt. Goose bumps
sprout across my skin, even though it's a hundred degrees
in here. "But I want to be there to see you smile. I want to
be the one smiling with you."

"I'm not quite sure what you're saying." Or maybe I
do, and I just don't want to get my hopes up.

"Me neither." He sighs, frustrated. "I just wish I could
experience all of it with you."

A glimmer of hope shines inside me. "Then experience
it with me."

"But how am I supposed to do that with all the stuff
going on?" Sadness consumes his face. "And what about
Sadie? How can I just bail on her?"

"You wouldn't be just bailing. You've helped a lot. And
you can still help." I step toward him until the tips of our
shoes brush. "You want to know how you do it? You just do
it—you just go. You say to hell with the faulty roof, flip it
the bird, and live your goddamn life."

"I wish it were that simple," he says quietly. "But no
one would ever let me just take off. And what if the Soul-

less Mileas chase me down? What if I put everyone in danger?"

"Those are all possibilities, but so is the police finding the people who are doing this to you. They could find Sadie. This could all be over soon. You never know. That's the thing, Ayden, you never know about anything. Just like you never know if you'll ever have a chance to do something like this tour again. It might be a once in a lifetime opportunity. And if you want to go, then we'll find a way. Don't let anyone take away your life from you." I hold my breath, waiting for him to agree that he'll do it. Go with me on this crazy three-month journey lying ahead of me.

He doesn't flat out say it, but he does faintly smile and the tension in his body unwinds.

"We'll talk to our parents and figure something out if you decide you want to do this," I say, trying not to get too hopeful. Not until he says it aloud. "But right now, there's something way more important we need to do."

His forehead furrows as he stares at me. "And what's that?"

A wicked grin rises on my face as I haul him toward the door. "We need to go jump in the ball pit. Like, right now."

He laughs as I drag him out of the bathroom and through the restaurant. I don't slow down as we race for the ball bit. I just hold on until the edge and then jump.

# Ayden

❦

We land in the ball pit, holding hands, and sink into a sea of plastic balls. When our feet hit the floor, Lyric laughs and pushes up to the top, like she's swimming in water.

"I always loved playing in these when I was a kid," she says as she twirls around in a circle, creating a funnel.

"I've never actually been in one," I admit as I pick up a ball and chuck into the air like a baseball.

"Well, now you can't say that anymore." She moves over by me. "Tell me one of your secret wishes."

I cock a brow at her. "One of my secret wishes?"

She nods, her green eyes sparkling. "I used to play this game with my dad when I was a kid. He would tell me his secret wish, then I'd tell him mine." She grins deviously. "He once told me that he secretly wished he could be a superhero for a day and wear a cape. I think he just said that, though, because he was trying to keep his wish PG."

I snort a laugh. "Why would I tell you my secret wish when you just outed your dad's?"

"Because you love me." Her bottom lip juts out and she bats her eyelashes at me as she clasps her hands in front of her. "Pretty please, Shy Boy."

I shake my head, but she's too damn adorable, and I can't help but smile. "You know that I know you do that on purpose, right?"

"Do what?" she asks innocently.

I touch the finger to her bottom lip. "Pout to get your way."

"Then why do you give me my way still?"

"Because I love giving you your way," I admit with a shrug. "I guess that's my secret wish. That I could always give you your way all the time. That I could give you what I know you want."

"You mean with the tour?" She catches my hidden meaning.

I nod. "I'm going to try to go for you, but I can't promise anything."

"Don't try for me." She loops her arms around me, angles her head back, and looks up at me. "Try for yourself."

Her long, blonde hair veils down her back, her green eyes glisten in the light, and her chest is pressed against mine. She looks so fucking beautiful right now, I could write a song about it.

*Eyes so green*
*That carry love for me.*
*How is that even possible?*
*How can something so beautiful*
*Be in love with some like me?*
*And her lips, so perfect*
*I can't taste enough of them.*

*And when she touches me,*
*It's too fucking complicated to breathe.*

"I'll try for both of us," I tell her. "Just as long as you do something for me."

"And what's that?"

"Kiss me—"

She crashes her lips to mine before I can even get the words out. Our tongues tangle as we sink into the pit. My hand skates down her side to her thigh and I lift her leg up and hitch it over my hip. She moans against my mouth as she grinds against me. I knot my fingers through her hair, feeling so comfortable being with her it's mind blowing. Just like the other night when she put her hands on me. It was the first time I ever allowed someone to touch me like that, and it was terrifying and incredible at the same time.

"Mom, Lyric and Ayden are making out in the ball pit!" Fiona announces as she steps up to the edge of the pit and points at us.

I softly toss a plastic ball at her, and she laughs, skittering out of the way.

"One day, when you're making out with your boyfriend," I tell her, "I'm going to get you back for that."

Fiona sticks out her tongue then skips off toward the game machines.

I spot Ethan and Mr. Scott heading our way. I don't think they're coming to yell at us for making out, but I'm not about to keep kissing Lyric when her dad could see us.

I sigh. "I guess that puts an end to our ball pit fun."

"You know they know we kiss, right?" Her brows arch. "In fact, I'm pretty sure they think we're having sex already, since my mom found that safe sex pamphlet in my nightstand drawer."

My lips part in shock. "She—You didn't—You told her we weren't having sex, didn't you?"

"I told her we weren't *yet*," she says. "But I've always been pretty close with my family, and I felt like I needed to tell her," she shrugs, "That we're getting really close to that point. At least I think we are."

I cast an unnerved glance at her dad as he busts up laughing at something Ethan says. "Does your dad know too?"

"My mom and dad tell each other everything, so maybe." She tosses a ball aside then lines her chest with mine. "Would you relax? They know we're in love, and that we aren't just two teenagers getting their freak on."

"You told them we're in love?" I whisper, a mixture of fear and nerves.

"Not yet. But I'm sure they can tell. I should probably tell them, though." Her head angles to the side as she muses over something. "It's actually my secret wish. That I could shout it out right now and everyone could celebrate the love with us." She jumps up and presses a kiss to my lips.

She hasn't smiled like this in a while, and it makes me so fucking relieved to see her happy like this.

My lips turn upward. "Well, how can I argue with that?"

"Really?" she asks, her eyes light up.

I nod, a knot twisting in my gut. "Yeah, go ahead."

"Hey everyone!" She shouts with laughter ringing in her voice. "I love this beautiful boy right here. And guess what? He loves me too!"

I can't bring myself to look in the direction of Ethan and Mr. Scott. "I feel sick," I mutter.

"My declaration of our love is no reason to get sick," she says, playfully pinching my arm. "Now cheer up. This is a good thing."

"Do they look mad?" I whisper with my head ducked.

She stands on her tiptoes and peers over my shoulder. "No, but they're headed over here." Lyric's eyes sparkle mischievously as she returns her gaze to me. "We could always sink to the bottom and hide from them."

I nod. "Yes, please."

She takes my hand. "Ready. One … Two … Three …"

We jump up then dive down, pressing our lips together.

# Lyric

The entire next day I'm so nervous and twitchy, people probably think I'm a spazz. But I can't help it. Today is an exciting day for everyone in my band. I just wish we didn't have that giant cloud constantly hovering over our heads, reminding us that a rainstorm could come at any moment.

Around two o'clock I head off to record my first album, and spend the next few hours with Ayden and my band at Infinitely Studio, my dad's recording studio, starting our career. We don't record every song that'll be on our album in one night, but we are planning to return within the next week to finish. Before we clock out for the day, I make sure Ayden and I do a duet, because, in my opinion, it's the best part.

"Are you sure you want to do this?" Ayden asks me as we prepare to go in and sing the song we wrote. "Because you can always back out."

"No way am I about to back out on one of my

dreams." I plant my butt on the stool and put my head-phones on, motioning Ayden to do the same.

He nervously sits down, slides on a set of headphones, and situates his guitar on his lap. I collect my guitar and get comfortable, disregarding Sage and Nolan gawking at us through the window.

"Ready?" My dad's voice floats through the speakers.

Ayden's been extremely jumpy around my dad, ever since I belted out that we were in love, and he flinches at the sound of my dad's voice. I don't know why he's acting all squirrely. No one has brought up our love declaration, except for my mom and she seemed pretty happy about it.

"I'm so glad you can just say it like that," she said to me as she worked on a painting in her studio at our house. "I had such a hard time expressing my emotions when I was younger."

"Really?" I was shocked because, for as long as I could remember, her and my dad have been happy and in love and not afraid to show the world.

She set the paintbrush down, nodding. "I had a lot of problems when I was younger. Thankfully, your dad stuck with me while I worked through them."

I couldn't help but think of Ayden and myself. He struggles sometimes with his emotions, but I'll never, ever give up on him. I want him. Forever.

I blink back to reality and lock eyes with Ayden. "Are you ready?"

He nods, his gaze fused to mine. "Whenever you are."

"We're ready whenever you are, daddy-o," I say through the microphone.

My dad gives me the go ahead, and I strum the first chord. Ayden follows my lead, and we play a few more chords, completely in sync, before I open my mouth and pour out my soul to the microphone.

"I never knew it could be like this, never thought such desire was possible, kissing the air from his lungs." My heart hammers in my chest. "And the heavens rain stars down on us, pieces of shimmering gold around us, pouring warmth all over us. Kiss me until I can no longer breathe. Raveling me up with you until I can hardly think. God, please fucking kiss me before I crumble to pieces."

We strum a few more chords, keeping the beat soft until it's Ayden's turn to come in. He summons a breath then opens his mouth and kisses the world with the beautiful sound of his voice.

"You make me weak. You make me strong. You make me ache. You make me feel so wrong. You make me burn for just a taste." His gaze burns into me, scorches my soul. "You make me, make me, so fucking insane. I can't stand it anymore. I want you all the time. It's always on my fucking mind. Please, just let me have you. God, please just say yes."

I nod. I don't even know why, other than I want him to have me.

He keeps his eyes on me until the song is finished.

I'm so riled up, I'm actually sweating.

My dad walks in, but I barely register what he's saying. I'm too caught up in Ayden, the sound of his voice, singing with him, singing one of *our* songs.

"You guys did a great job." My dad congratulates us with a huge-ass smile on his face. "Seriously, I'm not really a fan of duets, but that was pretty amazing."

"Thanks, Dad," I say, my gaze never wavering from Ayden.

My dad says a handful of other things about coming back in next week, but I hardly hear a word.

"Lyric, did you hear me?" my dad asks, looking at me with concern.

I blink my attention from Ayden and attempt to focus on my dad. "Nope. What's up?"

He sighs, sinking into a stool. "I asked if you want me to drive you home."

"We can just drive ourselves," I say as I slide off the stool to put my guitar in the case. "I know you have stuff to do."

"I'd rather you not drive home alone," he replies, crossing his arms. "It's late."

"I thought you had a meeting," I remind him. "That's what your secretary said when we came in here. And we won't be all alone. The officer will be following us."

"Yeah, I know." He frowns, actually pouting. "I forgot about the meeting. I wanted to take you out for ice cream or something."

"You can do it tomorrow," I suggest as I lock up my guitar case. "I can even clear my super busy schedule, just for you."

That cheers him up. "All right. I'll think of something fun to do." He turns to Ayden. "You can come too, if you want."

I smile as I tie my plaid over shirt around my waist.

*You just got mad cool points, Dad.*

Ayden glances at me, and I mouth, *come with us.*

"Sure. That sounds good, Mr. Scott." He picks up his guitar case.

"Call me Micha, okay," my dad insists. "Mr. Scott makes me feel so old."

"You kind of are old," I say. When he shoots me a nasty look, I add, "But the coolest old man ever."

He laughs, opening up the door. "Come on. This old man needs to get to work."

After we say goodbye to my dad, Ayden and I walk outside with Sage and Nolan to the parking lot. It's later in the evening and the sky is splashed with pink, orange, and gold.

"We so rocked today." Sage fist-bumps Ayden. "If we can sound like that on the tour, there's no doubt we'll get more tour offers."

Nolan tosses his drumsticks into the backseat of Sage's truck. "We did sound fucking awesome today, but what're we going to do when we have a sucky guitarist instead of Ayden?"

"Don't start," Sage warns, leaning against the back of his truck. "I already hear enough of that shit from Lyric."

"That's because it's the truth," I say, pulling my hair up as the heat instantly gets to me.

"Would you guys please stop arguing?" Ayden asks, shocking the three of us.

"Sorry, man," Sage says, holding up his hands. "I was just pointing out that they can complain about it all they want, but it doesn't fix the problem that we're going to be short a guitarist on the first fucking tour we got hired for."

"I'm sure they don't all suck," Ayden says, glancing at the screen of his phone.

Nolan shakes his head. "Yeah right. They're freaking terrible. Seriously. I've started wearing earplugs so I don't go deaf from the God awful noise they think is music."

"You wear earplugs?" I narrow my eyes at him and put my hands on my hips. "So not fair."

93

Sage sighs, retrieving a pack of cigarettes from his pocket. "You know, you could still change your mind, Ayden." He pops a cigarette between his lips, cups his hand around his mouth, and lights up.

Nolan perks up, rubbing his hands together. "Yeah, you could always do that. Make our lives easier."

Ayden fiddles with the leather bands on his wrists while staring at the ground. Sensing his uneasiness, I grab his hand. "We need to get home," I tell Sage and Nolan. "See you guys tomorrow."

Their moods deflate as they turn and get into Sage's truck. Ayden and I hop into his car without saying anything and he pulls out onto the busy road. I ignore the headlights of the cop car following us, and instead focus on stroking Ayden's palm during the entire drive to our neighborhood.

'That feels good," he murmurs as he steers the car into our subdivision.

"Yeah?" I brush my fingers across his skin again, tickling him softly.

He nods, his eyelashes fluttering. "It's relaxing."

"Maybe when we get home, I can give you a massage," I tease with a wink.

"Maybe," he says, surprising the crap out of me. He turns his head and our gazes weld. "What?" he asks. "Why are you looking at me like that?"

I keep looking at him the same way. "Looking at you like what?"

"Like you were when you…" His Adam's apple bobs up and down as he swallows hard. "Like you were when we were singing."

I rest my head against the seat, keeping my eyes on

him. "Maybe because I feel the same way as I did when we were singing."

He grows silent as he turns the car into the driveway of his house. The lights are off, but my house is lit up and music is blaring.

"My mom's having a party," I tell him, unfastening my seatbelt.

"I know," he says, turning off the engine and head-lights. "Lila told me about it earlier when she texted me and told me I could either go over to your house and wait for them to get home from Everson's practice. Or I could go inside my house, lock the doors, and set the alarm. But if I did that, I'm supposed to text her and let her know so she could give the police a heads up to keep an extra eye on me."

"How long is everyone going to be gone at practice?"

"At least until ten or so." He shrugs, looking over his shoulder at the police car parked in front of his house. "I guess there's a team barbeque after the practice."

For some insane reason, I think about that silly pamphlet tucked away in my dresser drawer. I don't know why it crosses my mind. Okay, maybe I do. "You want me to go to your house and wait with you? I'm sure my mom won't mind."

He stares at me, deciding his answer, before he unsteadily nods. My heart sprints so insanely I swear he can hear it.

We climb out of the car, meet around front, and link hands as we hike up the driveway. Once we get inside, Ayden texts Lila that he's home then we go up to his room and shut the door.

I turn around and face him, trying to figure out the

right thing to say other then, *hey we should get our freak on.* I shake my head at myself. Seriously, I've been listening to Maggie way too much. For all I know, Ayden's thoughts aren't even headed in the same direction as mine.

He sets his guitar case down on the floor then glances around his room. "You want to watch a movie?" he asks me, his cheeks looking flushed.

*Okay, so we're definitely not on the same page.*

"Sure." I kick off my boots and flop down on his bed, trying to appear more composed than I am. "What are you thinking? Horror? Romance? A comedy? Or Rom Com?" I smirk wickedly, because Ayden hates Rom Coms.

He studies me, touching his fingers to his lips. "I don't know… Whatever you want to watch, I guess."

"How about no movies and just…" Something about the way he's looking at me, with hunger in his eyes, gives me the courage to get to my feet, walk up to him, and brush my lips against his. I half expect him to pull away— it's always a fifty-fifty chance with him. Instead, he deepens the kiss, groaning as he backs me toward the bed.

"We don't have to do anything if you don't want to," he whispers between our fervent kisses. "I don't want you to feel pressured."

My stomach does a flip as I smile against his lips. "You know I never do anything I don't want to do."

"I know… I just want this to…" His voice sounds strained. "For you to… For this to be perfect for you."

"Trust me. It already is." I collide my lips with his, and the kiss goes from slow and savoring, to reckless and nervous.

We fall clumsily onto the mattress and I giggle as our

teeth clank together. He laughs, but the mood instantly turns serious again as he slips his tongue into my mouth.

I whimper as he bites my bottom lip, my back arching as I clutch onto his shirt, pulling him closer. His hands travel all over the outside of my shirt before I move back and pull it off. His fingers slide down my stomach and to the top of my jeans, and he fumbles with the button then the zipper.

By the time he strips me bare, I'm so nervous I'm shaking.

"A-are you sure you're okay?" he asks, his voice wobbly, unsteady, completely Ayden.

I nod, staring up at him. "I don't have anything though... Do you?"

He hesitates then gets up and walks to his dresser. When he returns, his shaky hand is carrying a condom.

"When did you get that?" I ask, trying to conceal my laughter over how guilty he looks that he has a condom.

He sighs, dropping the condom onto the bed as his eyes drink in every inch of me. "Lila made Ethan give some to me after they caught us fooling around that one time."

I prop up on my elbows, biting back a smile. "Well, as embarrassing as that must've been for you, I'm glad they did."

"You are?" His question isn't as simple as it sounds.

I nod then sit up and snag the hem of his shirt. He sucks in a sharp breath then raises his hands and lets me tug his shirt over his head. Once I get it off, I chuck it on the floor while he removes his jeans, leaving him only in his boxers. I take in the sight of him as I trace my fingers across his lean, but scarred stomach. I wish I could erase the pain of each one. Wish he never had to go through what he did.

*Wish. Wish. Wish.*

*Wish upon a star.*

*Wish and wish and wish.*

*You can spend all your time wishing.*

*But then you'd be missing out on this moment.*

He hooks a finger underneath my chin, bringing my attention to his eyes. He pauses, giving me time to back out. I'm not going to. Now that we're finally here in this moment, I never want to leave it.

"I-I love you." He leans forward and seals his lips to mine.

*I love you too.*

*More than anything, Ayden Gregory.*

*You are it for me.*

# Ayden

**I**'m terrified out of my fucking mind as I put a condom on, lie Lyric down on the bed, and situate myself between her legs. My thoughts are racing a thousand miles a second as I suck in a breath and start to slip inside her. My entire body quivers and it makes me feel pathetically weak. Thankfully, Lyric senses my nearing panic attack.

She cups my cheek. "Look at me," she whispers, steadily carrying my gaze. "We don't have to do this … Not if you're not ready."

"No, I want to. I-I want to be with you," I say, looking into her eyes. "I love you."

"I love you too," she whispers with small, nervous smile.

I take a breath, then another, before moving slowly inside her, not wanting to hurt her, and not wanting to lose it. Because the panic is there under the surface, threatening to take hold of me.

*I won't*

*Let it control me anymore.*
*This is my life.*
*This is where I want to be.*
*Only here.*
*With her.*

As I rock inside her, she holds onto my shoulders, staring up at me with complete trust. It's the most incredible thing I've ever experienced. And, while I'm still scared to death, I feel different. Changed. I never want to allow my fear to make me miss out on any other amazing moments like this. I've spent so much of my life missing out on the good stuff, because I allowed the bad stuff to consume me.

*No more.*
*Time to remove the cuffs from my wrists.*
*Time to free myself.*

An hour later, we're lying in my bed with our legs and arms tangled together. "This is for Keeps" by Spill Canvas is playing from the stereo, which I turned on because Lyric insisted this moment needed a song.

"I like this song," Lyric mutters as she rests her head against the crook of my shoulder.

I play with her hair as I gaze up at the ceiling, replaying what just happened between us. I'm still shocked that I wasn't dragged into an unwanted memory. It almost happened, but all I had to do was look at Lyric and the memory and fear faded.

"Are you sure you're okay?" Lyric props up on her arm and catches my gaze. "You've been really quiet."

"I'm fine." I sweep hair out of her eyes. "More than fine, actually."

She seems slightly insecure over something, which isn't like her. "You don't regret it, right?" she asks.

I swiftly shake my head. "Not at all. What happened …" The memory fills my mind of rocking inside her while kissing her deeply. "It was perfect."

"Good." She relaxes. "I need to write a song about this."

"About the first time we had sex?" I squeak, sounding pathetic.

"Don't freak out." She bites back a smile. "I won't use your name."

"It's not my name I'm worried about. I just want to be the only one who gets to see you like that."

"No one will see anything just from a song," she says, highly amused.

"That all depends on how descriptive you are."

"I won't be descriptive. I'll just write about how I feel."

"Which … Which is good, right?" I need to know—need to make sure she's okay with that just happened between us.

"Of course. What happened between us … It was really, *really* good." Even though she confidently maintains my gaze, a blush creeps across her cheeks. "We do get to do it again, right?"

My own cheeks heat as I nod.

We stare at each other for a heartbeat or two then I lift my head while pulling her against me, so our lips meet halfway. She groans from the connection as I grip her hip and roll her over, covering my body over hers. Right as things start to heat up again, though, my phone rings. I try to ignore it and continue exploring Lyric's mouth and body, but the damn thing won't shut up.

I grunt in frustration as I push back from Lyric.

She giggles as I climb off the bed to dig my phone out of the pocket of my jeans that are balled up on the floor.

"I love when you get frustrated like that," she says. "It's so adorable."

I smile at her as I swipe my finger across the screen. But when I see I've missed over ten calls from Lila, I frown.

"Shit, it's Lila … She's called a lot." I dial her number as I put my boxers on. "She's probably freaking out that I didn't answer."

"Ayden!" Lila cries before I can even get out a hello. "Why haven't you been answering your phone?"

"Sorry, Lyric and I were practicing some of our songs, and I didn't hear it ring," I lie as I pick up my jeans and slip them on.

"I'm just glad you're okay. I was worried sick. I even called the police and told them to check on you, so don't be surprised when the doorbell rings."

Right on cue, the doorbell echoes through the house.

"Who is that?" Lyric wonders as she gets out of bed and starts getting dressed.

I hold up my finger, indicating I'll be right back then I step out into the hallway heading for the stairway. "They just rang the doorbell," I tell Lila. "I'm headed down to tell them I'm okay. I'm really sorry I didn't answer."

"It's okay. It's okay." Her tone carries an edge.

I pause. "Is everything okay?"

She hesitates before she utters, "Ayden, the police found your sister."

A wave of fear and relief rushes through me. "They found her? Where was she? Is she okay?" I struggle to get air into my lungs.

*They found her.*

*But where?*

*Is she hurt?*

*Is she…*

"She's alive," Lila says. "I don't know the exact condition she's in, but you can meet me down at the hospital and we'll find out what's going on."

"Did they arrest anyone?" I can barely hear over my deafening heartbeat. "Did they catch my father?"

"They said they made some arrests, but I don't know all the details. When the detective called, he didn't say much, but I'll get more information from him when we get to the hospital."

"I'll head there right now." I hang up and my legs buckle out from under me.

"Ayden." Lyric appears beside me. Her eyes sweep across me, as if she's checking for visible wounds. "What happened?"

"They found Sadie," I manage to get out.

She kneels down on the floor in front of me, moving slowly, as if she's approaching a skittish cat. "Is she … Alive?"

I nod and that's when I lose it.

*Sadie is alive.*

*Sadie is alive.*

*She made it.*

*She survived.*

I start to cry and Lyric wraps her arms around me and rubs my back.

I cry even harder. For Sadie. For Felix. And for myself. Because for the first time in my life I don't feel so weighed down.

I don't want to think it, because it feels wrong to after spending so much time being chased by the Soulless Mileas, but maybe, just maybe this will finally all be over soon.

# Lyric

✿❀✿

"Lyric, why don't you help your dad in the kitchen while I finish saying goodbye to everyone," my mom says to me as I pace the foyer in my house, biting my fingernails.

I distractedly look up at her. "Huh?"

She heaves a sigh as she approaches me. "Honey, I know you're worried about Ayden, but wearing a hole through the floor isn't going to help."

"He said he'd text me and give me an update when he made it to the hospital." I check my phone again and frown when I see I have zero new messages. I wish I could've gone with him, but my mom and Lila didn't think that was a good idea since Ayden's going to be talking with the police. "He left over an hour ago." I tuck my phone away. "He has to be there by now."

"Honey, I'm sure he'll call you as soon as he can." She puts her hands on my shoulders and steers me toward the kitchen. "Now go get your mind off of stuff and help your dad clean up."

I begrudgingly go into the kitchen where my dad, Fiona, Everson, and Kale are cleaning up dirty dishes, food trays, and wine glasses left over from my mom's guests. Uncle Ethan dropped the three of them off about twenty minutes ago and then headed straight for the hospital. He didn't say much, but I could see the concern on his face when he mentioned needing to get an update on Sadie's condition. I worry how hurt she is. How much they broke her. She's been with them so long… God, it's hard to think about the stuff she must have been through.

I begin wandering around the house, picking up stray cups and plates while my mom urges guests toward the front door, trying to get them to leave as quickly as possible without seeming like a total douchebag about it.

"How are you holding up after what happened?" my dad asks as I return to the kitchen with a stack of plates.

"Fine." I set the plates down in the sink. "I'm just worried about Ayden and how he's handling this."

"I'm sure he's fine." He gives my shoulder a squeeze. "He's a strong person."

"Yeah, I guess that's true." I think about all the obstacles Ayden has overcome in his life, including the one I just helped him with only hours ago when we were in his room.

"Why do you look flushed?" My dad questions, studying me closely.

I lean back, hoping to God he can't see the answer on my face. He can barely handle the idea of me having a boyfriend. I can only imagine what he'd do if he found out I just had sex.

"I'm just a little hot. I think I'm going to go turn the air conditioning up." I round the kitchen island, heading for the thermostat in the hallway. When I reach it, I don't turn the air up, since I'm not really that hot.

I slump against the wall and take a minute to collect myself. I'm just about to go back into the kitchen when my phone vibrates. I dig it out of the pocket, so eager to read the message that I drop the phone on the floor.

"Shit." I pick it up and swipe my finger across the screen.

**Ayden: Hey, sorry I didn't text u sooner. Things have been crazy.**

**Me: But she's ok, right? I mean, your sister?**

**Ayden: I haven't seen her yet… I guess she had a broken arm that needed an operation. But the doctors said she should be fine. At least physically.**

I squeeze my eyes shut as tears sting my eyes. Poor Sadie. I can't believe people can be so cruel, so brutal, so ugly. The only thing that gets the tears to stop is that I remind myself there's also wonderful, amazing, beautiful stuff in the world. That not everything is bad.

**Me: Where did they find her?**

**Ayden: That's the strange part. She actually showed up at the police station.**

**Me: What???**

**Ayden: Yeah, she walked in and said who she was and that they let her go. Then she passed out. I guess the police had just raided the house she was being kept at and someone took off with her before she was found, but then they just dropped her off at the police station … It's so weird.**

**Me: That is really weird. Maybe the person**

who left her at the police station just panicked or something.

**Ayden: Maybe. I don't have all the details yet, but I should be talking to the detective soon. Hopefully, he won't try to pull that secretive shit and keep me in the dark about stuff.**

**Me: Let me know how it goes. And come see me as soon as you get home. I know it's only been a few hours since you left, but I miss you. I'm seriously going to turn into one of those needy girlfriends.**

**Ayden: I miss you too. I wish you were here with me. I'd probably be a lot more relaxed.**

**Me: I can try to relax you when you when you get back.**

**Ayden: That sounds nice.**

**Me: Good. It's a date then.**

For a split second, everything feels like it's going to be all right. Then another message pings through.

**Ayden: I have some bad news, though. The police made a lot of arrests, but as of now, they haven't found my dad.**

My fingers constrict around the phone. "Dammit."

**Me: What are they going to do?**

**Ayden: Keep looking for him. And I have to be watched by an officer at all times until they find him.**

My head slumps forward. I was so hopeful this was coming to an end, that Ayden was finally safe. But he'll never be until his dad's behind bars.

**Me: I'm sorry, Ay. I really am.**

**Ayden: I hate this.**

**Me: So do I. But they have to be closer to finding him, right? If they've found all those other people.**

**Ayden: I hope so... I just really want this to all be over.**

**Me: Me too.**

**Ayden: I have to go. The detective just showed up. Call u when I'm headed home. I love u.**

**Me: I love u too.**

With a heavy heart, I tuck the phone away and walk into the kitchen. Most of the plates and cups have been picked up and the air smells of lemon cleaner. Kale, Everson, and my dad have wandered off somewhere, but Fiona is at the table, munching on a cupcake.

"He's still sad," she remarks as I join her at the table.

I grab a cupcake off a platter and lick off a bite of frosting. "Who's still sad?"

She plucks a candy off the top of the cupcake and pops it into her mouth. "Ayden."

I peel the wrapper down and take a bite of the cake. "I don't think he's sad. Just stressed out."

"No, he's sad." She sets the cupcake on the table. "He's sad over his sister. And over you."

I freeze, mid bite. "Over me?"

She nods. "He's sad because he thinks he's going to lose you because he can't do stuff with you."

"Did you hear him say that?" I ask, trying not to get wigged out by her matter-of-fact attitude.

She simply shakes her head. "Nope, I felt it."

"You say that a lot. But I'm still not sure what you mean."

"It's hard to explain. And you probably wouldn't

believe me if I tried." She sits back in her chair and picks up the cupcake again. "My mom knew about me, though. It's why she gave me up. Because I was a weirdo."

Her words make me pause. I know Fiona's story. Know her mother was a drug addict and Fiona was taken away from her, so I have no idea why she just said what she did.

"Do you want to watch a movie or something?" I ask, hoping to get her mind off stuff.

"Nah, movies are lame." Her mood abruptly lifts. "You want to help me with this art project I'm working on? Maybe we could even get your mom to help with it."

"Sure." I scoot back from the table and stand up. "Just let me go change into my pajamas and then I'll meet you in the living room, okay?'

"Thanks, Lyric. You're the best." She heads for the living room, but stops in the doorway. "You're kind of like the sister I never had. And just think, when you and Ayden get married, you'll be my sister-in-law."

She skips out of the room, leaving me shaking my head.

Marriage. I'm so not ready for that yet. Maybe a ways down the road, in like five or six years. Still, just thinking about the future, the possibilities, gets me excited. I just need Ayden here with me.

When I reach my bedroom. I'm extremely distracted as I slip off my sandals and turn on the light, and it takes me a second to notice something's different about my room. At first, I can't place a finger on what it is, only that I have an uneasy feeling. I glance at the floor, at the window, then the walls. That's when I spot the circular symbol painted just above my bed. The same symbol that the Soulless Mileas tattooed on Ayden's side.

I spin for the door to run downstairs, but crash into a hard, solid object. I trip backwards and open my mouth to scream, but the man I ran into quickly bends down and slaps a hand over my mouth.

"It's so nice to finally meet you, Lyric." A grin spreads across his face.

Terror whips through me as I note the knife in his other hand, and I mentally calculate what I should do. There's no way I'm just going to give in to whatever he's planning on doing to me; no way I'm going down without a fight. So, I lift my leg to kick him right in the stomach, putting every ounce of strength I have in it.

He curses, falling down on me, and crushing me with his weight. But he recovers quickly and wrestles me to the floor. His hand slips from my mouth as he works to pin me down. I start to scream again, but he moves the knife to my throat.

"Don't give me a reason to kill you," he warns, his eyes darkening. "It would really make me angry, especially since I'm not the one who's supposed to kill you."

I swallow hard and the movement causes the blade to graze my skin.

He assesses me, then stands up, yanking me to my feet with him. Gripping me by the arm, he drags me to the dresser and cranks up the stereo so loudly I can't hear myself think—so loud no one can hear me scream.

"M-my parents are going to hear the music and come up here," I stammer as he grabs me by the hair.

He shakes his head. "You do this enough that they won't even give it a second thought."

Vomit burns at my throat. He's right. I've blasted my music for as long as I can remember, and my parents are so used to it by now that it hardly bothers them. What I don't get, though, is how he knows this.

"We need to get Ayden here," he says loudly over the music. "He's the one who's supposed to be doing this. He's the one who needs his soul cleansed."

I'm not quite sure what he's talking about, but I'm guessing it has to do with the Soulless Mileas and their ritual. My adrenaline skyrockets as panic sets in. *I need to get out of here. Now! Figure out a way, Lyric!*

"I have an idea," the man says thoughtfully as he backs me into the wall and lines the knife with my throat again. "Do you have your phone on you?"

Every instinct I have tells me to lie, so I shake my head.

His eyes darken and he roughly sticks his hand into my pocket and grabs my phone. A smile curls at his lips as he scrolls through my contacts and presses a few buttons.

While he's not paying attention, I seize the opportunity, bring my leg up, and knee him in the balls. He hunches over, gasping for air.

I bolt for the door, opening my mouth, "Help—"

I'm slammed from behind and shoved to the floor. I land hard on my face, but promptly flip over onto my back. The man jumps on me, his knee connecting with my stomach.

I gasp as the wind is knocked out of me.

"I guess it's going to be me, then." He pins my arms to the floor then raises his knife above his head.

I kick him again, refusing to give in, as I open my mouth to scream, praying someone will hear me.

# Ayden

❦

I'm standing in the busy waiting room of the hospital, waiting for my sister to get out of surgery while listening to Detective Rannali give me an update on what they're doing to find my father, when I get a text.

**Lyric: I have her. It's time to cleanse your soul, Ayden. And u better be a good son and come alone.**

It feels like a knife has been gashed into my heart, and I'm bleeding out from the inside. I can't breathe. Can't get oxygen into my lungs as I painfully realize what the note left in Lyric's locker meant.

"Ayden, what's wrong?" Lila jumps up from the chair she's sitting in and rushes to me.

"My dad... He has Lyric," I croak as I hand her my phone.

She reads the message and her skin drains of color. "Oh God. This can't be happening. No... no... no... "

Detective Rannali grabs the phone from Lila. "What's going..." He trails off as he reads the message. "Shit."

I spin around, pushing people out of my way as I run for the exit doors.

"Ayden! Wait!" Lila chases after me with Ethan tailing at her heels. "You can't go anywhere by yourself!"

I whirl around. "They have Lyric, Lila. I have to find her." I start to turn around, heading for the parking lot.

Her fingers fold around my arm and she forces me to stop. "We don't even know where she is."

"Then we have to find out—we have to find her." Reality crashes over me and I almost collapse to the ground.

*God, please don't let him hurt her.*
*I don't know what I'd do if I lost her.*
*I'd crumple into dirt.*
*Disappear into an eternity of darkness.*
*Fade away into nothing.*
*I don't care if it makes me seem weak.*
*Just thinking about living without her.*
*It's killing me.*

"We'll find her." Lila guides me back toward the doors. "But we need to be safe about it."

Ethan walks on the other side, staying close, like he's afraid I'm going to try to run off again. I want to. Want to get the hell out of here and find Lyric. No, not want. *Need.*

By the time we return to the waiting room, Detective Rannali has phoned in the report and is ready to take off somewhere.

"I need to call Micha and Ella," Lila mutters, staring into empty space, her eyes wide with fear. "Oh my God, what am I supposed to say to them?"

"I can do it," Ethan offers, retrieving his phone from his pocket.

"The Scotts are already informed of what's going on," Detective Rannali tells us as he picks up his suit jacket from a chair and slips it on.

"How were they already informed?" I match his stride as he takes off for the exit. "Did you just call them? What did they say?"

"They called the station about five minutes ago and reported a break in at their house," he says as the doors glide open. "I'm headed to their house now."

"Do you… Do know if Lyric's okay?" I ask as we step outside and head for his car.

"I'm not sure. I think they're still trying to detain the person who broke in."

"It's my dad." I smash my lips together as guilt crushes my chest. "The text said son."

He slams to a halt in the middle of the parking lot. "Ayden, you should probably stay here and wait for Sadie to get out of surgery."

I shake my head. "There is no fucking way I'm going to stay here until I know Lyric's okay." I want to be here for my sister, but I'll be useless until I'm one hundred percent certain Lyric's okay. "Lila and Ethan can stay here just in case she gets out before I get back. I *need* to go with you." More than I've ever needed anything in my entire life.

Detective Rannali glances back at the hospital, then sighs. "Fine, you can ride with me."

The drive to Lyric's house is long and painful. I'm so wound up that I half expect my heart to give out on the way there.

When we pull up into the neighborhood, flashing red and blue lights are lighting up the entire block.

Detective Rannali parks the car as close to the house as he can get, then he turns off the engine and reaches for the door. "Stay here until—"

I barrel out of the car before he can finish.

"Ayden, wait!" Detective Rannali shouts after me as I run for Lyric's house.

I weave past cop cars and neighbors who've gathered around to watch the scene. Officers have formed a small line and are trying to keep everyone back, so I veer left and duck through an unguarded area near the fence line.

I'm not sure where to go, so I head for the back door. Right as I reach the steps, two officers exit the house, hauling out a middle-aged man in handcuffs.

He has the same eyes and hair color as me, his face recognizable from the memory. "Let me go. I didn't do anything wrong," he spats to the officers. "You're the ones who are wrong, for stopping me." He's walking awkwardly, like it's painful to move his legs, and his face and eyes are swollen, like someone beat the crap out of him.

I grind to a halt as fear and rage storm through me. "Where is she?" I growl.

"Kid, you can't be here," one of officers warns me, gently pushing me to stay back.

I follow them as they drag my father down the driveway and to a police vehicle. "You better not have done anything to her!" I shout.

"I was never planning on doing anything to her. It was supposed to be you. Your soul needs the cleansing. Not mine. I've cleansed my soul many, many times." His smile expands as he ducks his head and the officer forces him into the backseat. "I thought you could use Sadie. That her death could cleanse her soul, but then I heard you and Lyric say you loved each other for the first time, and I knew Sadie couldn't be your sacrifice. It had to be Lyric."

I fucking hate hearing him say her name, but taking in his words is even worse. The only way he could've heard Lyric and I say I love you for the first time is if he was either in the bedroom with us, or he bugged the room. Either option is equally as sickening, and it takes every ounce of strength I possess not to push the officers out of the way and strangle him.

"You're so fucked up," I snap, moving back as an officer steps in front of me and blocks my way.

"You need to keep back," the officer warns, steering me away from the car.

"You're part of me," my dad calls out. "And don't you ever forget that. I'll get out of this and find you. I promise I will. We all will—"

The officer slams the car door, locking my dad in the backseat. I stare at him for a second or two longer before I turn my back on him and start searching for Lyric.

I'm an erratic mess of nerves and anxiety by the time I find her parents standing near the back of an ambulance, staring inside, looking sick to death. Terror crashes through me as I run toward them and look inside the ambulance.

Lyric is inside, sitting on a stretcher, being examined by an EMT. When she sees me, her eyes light up, and she leaps to her feet, ignoring the EMT's protests.

"I've never been so glad to see you in my life," she says as she jumps into my arms and wraps her legs around me.

"Tell me you're okay," I beg as I clutch onto her for dear life.

She leans back to look me in the eye. "I'm fine. Just a few scratches, but it's mostly just carpet burn."

I carefully set her down, but only so I can examine every inch of her. She might have said she was okay, but I need to be absolutely certain. I don't see any wounds other than a few scrapes on her legs. Her eyes are a bit swollen, but I think that might be from crying.

"Ayden, relax." Her fingers caress my cheek, bringing my attention to her eyes. "I'm fine. I swear."

"What happened?" I swallow hard, my voice thick with emotion.

*My body starts to shake*
*Breathing in her words.*
*The truth is potent.*
*The truth is raw.*
*The truth is real.*
*That I could have lost her.*

She sighs exhaustedly. "He snuck into my room, used my phone to text you, then I kicked the crap out of him until he let me go. I think he had bigger plans, but after about ten kicks to the balls, he could barely breathe. Then my dad came in and beat the shit out of him..." Her muscles stiffen and her voice drops to a whisper. "For a second, I was worried he wasn't going to stop... That my dad was going to kill him."

A sick, twisted part of me wishes that had happened. But the last thing I want is for Lyric's dad to have blood on his hands.

"You're so fucking strong," I whisper, on the verge of sobbing. "And I'm so sorry you had to go through that—through any of this."

"Don't be sorry," she says firmly. "Just be glad, okay. That's all you need to be right now."

"About what?"

"That it's over."

It takes a moment for the full impact of her words to sink in. Then I pull her against me, promising myself I'll never let her go again.

# Ayden

❧❀❧

After my father is arrested, the police spend the next day ransacking the Scott's and my house for any hidden cameras and recording devices. They find a few in Lyric's room and in my room. The idea that he was watching us makes me sick to my stomach, but like with everything else, it's something I just have to work on getting past.

As the rest of the week goes by, things slowly start to return to normal. Lyric and I spend most of our time attached at the hip, working on songs and simply relaxing, something we haven't been able to do in a while.

"You're staring again," she says to me while we're lounging around in her bed.

Her shirt is rolled up and her long legs are tangled with mine as we work on a new song. A little Nirvana is playing from the stereo, which brings back memories of the first day I met her. We also have all the windows open, mostly because we feel safe enough to have them open, and a warm summer breeze is blowing into the room.

"I'm sorry," I say, sounding very unapologetic. "I guess it's the song. It reminds me of the first day I met you and how I couldn't stop staring."

Her lips twitch with amusement. "Aw, the staring days. How can I forget those?"

"I was such a weirdo. Who knows why you became friends with me."

"Um, hello, because I'm a weirdo too. And as a fellow weirdo, your weirdoness barely fazed me."

I chuckle. "Well, I'm glad."

We grow quiet as we listen to the song, and my thoughts drift to everything that's happened over the last couple of years.

So much bad has existed in my life, yet there's been so much good stuff. Sometimes I got so lost in the bad that I couldn't see all the good, but I don't want that to be the case anymore. I want to experience my life. Breathe in every good moment.

"Tell me what you're thinking," Lyric whispers as she scoots closer to me.

"I'm thinking about how much you mean to me and how great you've made my life." I set down the pen I'm holding so I can drape my arm over her side. "And how I never want to lose you. How I want to spend the rest of my life experiencing good stuff with you to make up for all the bad things we've been through."

She chews on the end of her pen, a pucker forming between her brows. "That sounds nice. Really, really nice. And I hope it happens. I hope we get to spend a lot of time with each other doing all sorts of crazy things."

"It'll definitely happen." I smooth my thumb between her brows. "What's with the worried look?"

Hesitancy masks her expression. "I was thinking about your sister, actually… You're going to see her today, right?"

I nod, glancing at the clock. "I'll probably have to leave pretty soon."

I've visited Sadie a couple of times over the last few days, but every time I go there, she's asleep. The doctors say she doesn't sleep very well, so no one's supposed to disturb her when she's out.

Lyric sits up, pulling me with her, then crisscrosses her legs. "Do you know what you're going to say to her if you get to talk to her today?"

I shake my head, closing my notebook. "I've gone over it in my head for years, what it was going to be like when I saw her again. I just never pictured it being in this kind of situation."

"I'm sure you'll do great." She gives my hand a reassuring squeeze. "And I think Sadie will probably just be happy to see you."

"But what if she's not?" I whisper. "What if she blames me for not finding her?"

"That's not going to happen, because it's not true. What happened wasn't your fault. It was *those people*." Her expression hardens.

"It might not be my fault, but I promised her I'd find her, and the fact that I didn't feels like I failed her somehow."

"You didn't fail anyone." She yawns. "And I have a feeling Sadie is going to agree with me."

"That's because you're an optimist." I laugh at her as she yawns again. "What's up, sleepy head?" I suddenly grow worried. "Wait, have you been having trouble sleeping?"

She stretches her arms above her head, her back arching. "No. I've been staying up late working on some new songs. I know it's morbidly twisted, but after everything that happened, my creativity sparked a freaking ton. I have so many ideas sloshing around in my brain that I don't even know what to do with it." She lowers her hand to her lap. "You want to read the song I wrote about that one night?"

"About the night my dad broke in?" I ask warily.

She shakes her head. "No, about the first time we had sex."

My body ignites with desire and need as I remember that night and the other nights we've spent together since.

"Hey, don't give me that look; otherwise I might start kissing you and we know where that leads." She points her finger at the open door. "And as much as I want things to lead in that direction, both of our parents are downstairs." She grins. "However, if you want, I can totally get some alone time later."

Just thinking about being alone with her causes my pulse to throb. "I definitely want that."

"Good." She leans in and brushes her lips against mine. "Now, do you want to read my song?"

I steal another kiss. "Of course."

Grinning from ear to ear, she flips open her notebook and sets it on my lap, pointing at which page to read.

*Our bodies wind*
*Creating the perfect song*
*As your lips fuse to mine.*
*I could do this all night long.*
*Lie here*
*Tangled up with you.*

.   .   .

S o closely
        No one will know
        Where you start
And where I end.


M y heart is pounding
        With every stolen kiss
        My mind is racing
Longing for a wish
That we could stay like this.
Always.


S o closely
        No one will know
        Where you start
And where I end.


T his moment with you,
        God it's branded in my mind.
        I want to keep it forever
Trap it inside
So it'll always be mine.
Forever.

.   .   .

S *o closely*
*No one will know*
*Where you start*
*And where I end.*

"I want to sing it one day during a concert," she announces after I'm done reading it. "I won't do it, though, unless you promise to sing it with me."

I think she might be secretly asking a question without actually having to say it aloud. But I can't promise her I'll go on the tour yet. Not until I find out what's going to happen with Sadie. As of now, I have no clue what kind of condition she's in, and she doesn't even have a place to live. And I need to be here for her while all that is out.

"Maybe one day we can sing it," I say, shutting the notebook.

"Okay. Just as long as it definitely happens." She tries not to frown. "Tonight we're playing at my dad's club with a guy that Sage wants to be our new guitarist. You should come so you can see how bad we suck. Maybe you can give him a few pointers."

I can't contain my laughter.

"Hey, I'm not trying to be funny." She playfully pinches my side.

"I know you're not." My laughter dies down. "It's just the first time I've seen you be so pessimistic about something."

"Music is my life, and so is the band," she tells me. "And this guy makes us look like amateurs. We're going to be booed off the stage."

"I'm sure that won't happen."

"At least promise you'll be there tonight in case it does, so I can have a shoulder to cry on."

"Okay, I'll be there." I don't believe for a second that they'll be booed off stage, but if she needs me to be there then I will.

"Now kiss me, before you have to leave," Lyric demands, leaning in.

We steal a few more kisses before Lila shouts up the stairs that it's time to go.

"See you tonight," I tell Lyric as I collect my stuff and climb off the bed.

She nods, her lips swollen from my kisses. "Text me if you need anything. Even if it's just to talk."

I promise her I will, then I meet Lila and Ethan downstairs and we head out to the car.

On the way to the hospital, Lila asks me at least ten times how I'm doing. Like always, I tell her that I'm okay, but this time, I actually am. Yeah, I still have nightmares sometimes and there are moments when I cry, mostly when I think about my brother's death and Sadie in the hospital. Even my mother's death gets to me. But for the first time in my life, I actually feel free from the past now that it's behind bars. There are tons of charges against the people who tortured my siblings and me; charges ranging from murder to kidnapping. Detective Rannali assures me they have a solid case, which should keep my father and his followers there for a very long time.

"Ayden, we wanted to talk to you about something before we go in," Lila says to me after she parks the car in the hospital parking lot.

It's midday and the sun shines through the windows, heating up the car the moment she turns off the engine.

"What's up?" I ask, confused by how nervous she seems.

She trades a look with Ethan, and he twists around in the passenger seat to look at me,

"It's about your sister," he says to me. "And her coming to stay with us after she's released from the hospital."

"Detective Rannali was the one who suggested it," Lila explains, unbuckling her seatbelt. "But Ethan and I had already talked about it... I know she's seventeen and is almost a legal adult, but with everything she's been through..." She smashes her lips together, fighting back the tears. "We just thought it'd be nice if she had a place to call home."

Even though I try to fight them back, a few tears manage to escape my eyes. I want to say so much to them. Thank them for everything, for giving me a home, for not giving up on me when things got hard. For giving me a family. But I'm so choked up, I can only manage a nod as I scoot forward and wrap an arm around her.

She gasps in shock, because I normally don't hug.

"Thank you." I suck back the tears. "And I mean that. Thank you for everything."

"You don't need to thank us for anything," she says. "You're our son, and we'll always be here for you."

We hug for a second longer before I move away. I clear my throat a few times and reach for the door to get out of the car.

As we walk into the hospital and toward Sadie's room, I go over in my head what I'll say to her if she's awake. It'll be the first time I've talked to her in almost five years and for some of those years, she was locked up in a house with people who tortured her. I worry there won't be any of that spunky, lively, carefree sister that I grew up with, and I won't have a damn clue what to say to her.

"Oh my goodness, she's awake," Lila says after she peers into Sadie's room. She steps back and turns to me. "We'll let you go in first and talk to her, okay? So we don't overwhelm her."

Nodding, I take a breath and step inside.

Sadie is sitting in the bed when I enter, staring out the window with a strange look on her face, like she's deeply contemplating something. She must hear me walk in, because she turns her head and looks over her shoulder at me.

We both freeze and just stare at each other.

She looks different, yet the same; her brown hair is still long and her face is covered with freckles. But there's a cast on her arm and a scar on her cheek, remnants that she's not the same Sadie I knew five years ago. That she's been beaten and tortured and God knows what else.

After a second or two goes by, I open my mouth to ask her if she knows who I am, but then she's already running to me.

"Oh my God, I thought I was never going to see you again," she cries as she wraps her good arm around me.

I start crying again, and it's ridiculously embarrassing. I seriously need to get a grip on myself. But the fact that she's here and alive, it's so fucking overwhelming I can't stop the tears from flowing.

She trembles as she hugs me, and I can sense that fear inside her, the fear of being touched. But she must be stronger than I was, because she keeps holding onto me.

"I'm so sorry," I say through my tears.

She shuffles back, giving me a quizzical look. "Sorry for what?"

"For not finding you." I wipe tears from my cheeks with the sleeve of my shirt. "I tried. I tried so fucking much, but no matter what I did, it all led to a dead end."

Her eyes pool with tears. "You didn't find me because they didn't want you to find me. There was nothing you could've done. As long as our..." Anger and fear flash in her eyes and her hands tremble as she balls them into fists. "As long as *he* wanted me there, I was always going to be there."

"How long..." I breathe in and out, trying to keep myself from crying again. "How long were you there?"

She turns her back to me, wrapping her arms around herself. "Ayden, I don't want to talk about this." She climbs back onto the bed with her feet dangling over the edge. "I've spent too much of my life surrounded by this shit, and now that I've finally gotten out, everyone just wants me to sit around and talk about what happened. I don't want to. All I want to do is forget about everything."

"I get what you're saying." I pull a chair up and sit down. "I forgot about what happened to us for a while and thought it was easier that way."

"You forgot?" she asks, her eyes widening. "Really?"

I nod. "Up until a few weeks ago, I couldn't remember any of the time we were in that house together."

"You're lucky then," she mutters, her shoulders slumping.

"I'm not so sure about that," I mumble. When she gives me a confounded look, I add, "I couldn't remember because I was repressing everything, but it wasn't healthy."

"So you're saying you're happier now that you can remember?" she asks, confused.

"I still can't remember everything now, but what I did remember helped them track the people down." I slant forward in the chair and rest my arms on my knees. "I've learned over the past couple of years that running away from your feelings only allows them to grow and feed off you, and eventually they'll nearly kill you if you don't learn to deal with them."

"You sound just like I remember," she says softly, almost smiling. "You always had a poetic way of saying things."

"I did?"

She nods. "You did. It was always fun listening to you talk when you got really passionate about something."

"I'm glad there were fun times … Sometimes when I look back at the past, all I can see is darkness."

"There were a few good times I can remember …" She trails off as she scoots back in the bed and rests against a pillow.

"Are you tired?" I ask, getting ready to stand up and leave. "Maybe I should let you sleep."

She shakes her head and motions for me to sit down. "I don't want to be alone. But I don't want to talk about the past right now. I know you say it's not healthy, but I just can't yet, okay?"

If that's what she wants, then that's what I'll give her. "What do you want to talk about then?"

"You." A trace of a smile rises on her face, but pain and fear haunts her eyes. "I want to hear all about your happy new life."

"How do you know it's been happy?" I wonder curiously.

"Because I can see it in your eyes," she says with a shrug.

"It hasn't always been that way, though."

"Then start from where it does get happy."

I rack my mind for the moment in my life where things turned around for me, where happiness felt within reach. "Well, I was adopted by this really amazing family," I say with a smile as I remember the day the Gregorys brought me home.

"Oh yeah?" She rotates on her side, cradling her casted arm. "Are they the ones who keep peeking through the doorway?"

I glance over my shoulder right as Lila walks by, trying to look casual as can be. I chuckle under my breath, turning back to Sadie. "That's Lila ... My mom, I guess." It's strange to say that to Sadie, to call someone else other than our real mother my mom.

"She seems worried about you," she says. "She's walked past the room about a thousand times."

"That's just how she is." I pause, debating whether to tell her what Lila and Ethan told me in the car. "They want you to come live with us."

Her brows shoot up. "*What?* They can't ... There's no way they'd want ..." Her eyes water up again.

My heart aches at her self-doubt, the feeling of unworthiness of having something good.

"I think you should live with them," I tell her. "They're really nice people who'll help you get through this."

"Did they ... Did they help you?"

"They did," I say. "And so did Lyric."

Her forehead creases. "Who's Lyric?"

How do I even begin to explain who Lyric is? The girl I'm in love with? No, she's more than that. Way, way more.

Not knowing how else to explain it to her, I start from the beginning, telling her about my journey with the Gregorys and how I fell in love with my best friend.

"So … you're in love?" Sadie asks after I'm finished.

I nod, fiddling with the leather band Lyric gave me. "I am."

She blinks, trying to hold the tears back, but they pour out of her eyes. "I'm so happy for you. I really, really am. I was so worried that maybe we both ended up broken and ruined but … Seeing you like this … "

I scoot forward in the chair and place an unsteady hand over hers. "I'm sorry. I didn't mean to make you cry."

"No, it's fine. I'm glad you did … And I'm glad you fell in love." She sniffles. "It gives me hope that maybe I'm not completely broken … That if you can make it, maybe … Maybe I can too."

It takes all I have in me not to break down and sob. "Sadie, you're going to make it. I swear to God you will. And I'll be there for you."

She cries for another minute or two before she pulls it together. "I don't want to cry anymore. Please, Ayden, tell me something that won't make me cry … Tell me more about your family… And Lyric … And this band and the tour… It all sounds so great." She sniffles as she dries her tears with the back of her hand. "I can't believe you ended up being musically talented. I remember when you tried learning how to play the flute. You sucked."

"Hey, I was eight," I protest. "And the only lessons I had were from Mr. Grangering. You remember him?"

"That grumpy old man that had a lot of cats," she says, nodding. "I didn't know he gave you lessons."

"The lessons really weren't that great since he got the harmonica confused with the flute. You should've seen him try to play it."

She laughs softly, but then her expression instantly plummets as terror flashes through her eyes. "I've always wanted to learn how to play the guitar … I thought about it a lot while I was … But I didn't think I'd ever be able to… Get the chance to."

"I can teach you," I offer.

"That would be amazing." She tries to smile but instantly frowns.

"Lyric can teach you how to play too," I offer, trying to keep the conversation going so she'll stay distracted from her thoughts. "She's actually just as good as me. Maybe even better."

"I want to hear her sing," she says. "When you were talking about it, all this excitement was in your eyes and I want to feel that excitement too."

"I'm sure there'll be plenty of chances for you to hear her."

"Maybe when you're on this tour thingy, I can go watch one of your concerts." Self-doubt seizes her expression as she grips onto the blanket for dear life. "W-well, just as long as I can stand backstage. I-I don't think I can stand being out in a crowd."

I completely understand where she's coming from. I remember the first concert I went to and how terrifying it was being in the crowd. Thankfully, Lyric was there with me and calmed me down.

"I'm not sure I'm going on the tour… I'm still deciding," I offer her a reassuring smile. "But you can definitely watch me play sometime."

"It's not because of me, is it?" she asks worriedly.

Not wanting to make her feel guilty over anything, I choose my next words carefully. "No, there's just some other stuff I need to do right now."

She shakes her head. "Ayden, please don't stop living your life because of me. I'm so jealous of what you have, and I'd die if I knew I ruined stuff for you."

"You're not ruining—"

She cuts me off, clutching onto my hand in desperation. "Promise me you won't. Promise me you won't change your life because I'm here now. I don't want you to do that."

"But I want to be there for you," I say, choking up. "I don't want you to go through this alone."

"I'm not telling you not to be there for me. I-I'm just telling you to live your life. We were given a second chance, so promise me you'll do everything you want to do. That you'll be happy."

"I'll promise to if you promise to."

"I'll try," she whispers. "I'm not going to let them break me."

She's stronger than I expected, but I can still see pain hidden under the strength, the internal battle trying to consume her. And I need to be there for her, to make sure it never completely takes hold.

I spend the next hour telling Sadie about my life, because she doesn't want to discuss anything else. Then Lila and Ethan come in and introduce themselves. Sadie seems skittish around them and acts even more erratic when a nurse comes in to do a check up on her and to tell us visiting hours are over.

"Remember what you promised," Sadie says to me as I'm walking out of the room.

I turn around and nod. "Just as long as you remember too."

She smashes her quivering lips together and nods before inching away from the nurse.

I hate leaving her alone, but she has to stay at the hospital for a few more days until she's made a full recovery.

Lila, Ethan, and I leave the hospital in silence. By the time we get to the car, it's late and the stars and moon are shining in the sky. Even though I might not make it in time, I ask Lila to drive me to Infinite Bliss so I can try to catch my band perform with their new guitarist.

As we make the drive across town, Sadie's words replay in my mind, the promise to be happy and live life. I know what that means, what makes me happy, but I want to be here for Sadie too and help her through what I know is going to be a hard time. Maybe, though, there's a way to do both.

"I have a favor to ask you guys," I say to Lila and Ethan before we climb out of the car to go inside the club.

"You can ask us anything," Lila reminds me as she shuts off the headlights. "Well, within reason of our capabilities."

I nervously explain my idea to them and then hold my breath as I wait for their answer. Is this a good idea? Is this really what I should do? I don't know if it is or not, but I guess I'm doing it.

Ethan glances at Lila with his brow raised. "What do you think?"

She shrugs then smiles. "I think he deserves it."

"All right, Ayden, you have yourself a deal," Ethan tells me with a grin. "Man, I'm so jealous. I've always wanted to go on a tour."

"Why didn't you?" I ask as I reach for the door handle.

"Because he hates crowds," Lila answers for him.

Ethan gives a shrug. "It's true. I never could get past all those damn people crammed into a room, sweating all over each other."

His statement does not surprise me, and honestly, I kind of understand where he's coming from.

"Thank you for letting me do this," I say, opening the door.

"You deserve it," Lila replies as she collects her purse from the console. "Like I said, we'll always be here to help you. Don't ever forget that."

I have a smile on my face as I get out of the car, practically running as I head to tell Lyric the news.

# Lyric

I try not to pout that Ayden missed the set, but I'm a tad bit sulky. I know he had a good reason for not showing up, though. That more than likely his sister was awake and the two of them are talking. I hope everything went okay. That Sadie's doing okay. That Ayden's doing okay with the guilt I know he feels over what happened to her.

I dig out my phone, deciding to text him.

**Me: Hey! Just wanted to c how everything was going. I'm guessing that your sister was awake this time?**

He doesn't answer right away, so I put the phone into my pocket and head out of the backstage area and down to the floor. It's Friday night and the place is crammed with rowdy drunk people, dancing around, throwing back shots, and ordering drinks at the bar. We were the only live band playing tonight, so my dad has cranked up the music.

"Are you sure you just don't want to go home?" My dad shouts over the music as he struggles with whether or not to leave me out here alone. Ever since the thing with Ayden's dad happened, my mom and dad have been overly protective of me. I was actually worried they were going to try to stop me from going on tour. While they do seem a little more hesitant than they did before, they haven't tried to talk me out it. "Or I could stay out here with you and hang out?"

"I'm fine." I wave him off. "Go back to your office. I'm probably going to head home soon."

The bartender hands him a beer and my dad pops off the top. "Maybe you should come hang out with me."

"Dad, you have a meeting with the new band filling in for us," I remind him, dabbing my fingers under my eyes to fix my eyeliner that I know is smudged—it always is after I finish performing. "I probably shouldn't be in there while you guys discuss business."

"We could pretend you're my secretary," he suggests, checking the time on his watch.

"Dad, go, or you're going to be late." I shoo him toward the hallway. "I'll head home as soon as mom gets back from work." So I don't have to be in the house alone.

While Ayden's dad and many other members of the Soulless Mileas were arrested last week, I still feel unsettled, especially when I'm home alone. I went to a therapist the other day to talk, and I realized I might be more affected by what happened than I originally let on. The therapist told me we could have phone appointments while I'm on the road if I wanted to, and I agreed, just to make sure that the fear I feel will eventually fade and won't take control of my life.

After I finally convince my dad back to go to his office, I chill out on the balcony near the dance floor, trying to decide whether I want to dance yet or wait until I hear back from Ayden before I really let loose. Because I fully plan on dancing. Need to for the sake of my sanity.

"In just over a couple of weeks, we'll be on the road," Sage announces as he walks up to me. He's carrying a beer, and he has a dopey smile on his face, which probably means he's high. "Seriously, Lyric, why don't you look more excited?"

"I'm excited," I assure him, turning and resting my elbows on the railing. "I'm just thinking about some stuff. That's all."

Sage takes a swig of his beer then leans against the railing, staring at our new guitarist who's flirting with a woman twice his age. "Yeah, right. You're so full of shit. I know it's because Ayden's not here."

Not wanting to talk about Ayden not being part of the band anymore, I point at the beer in his hand. "Dude, you know you can't drink that in front of my dad. He's chill, but not that chill."

"I'll put it down if he comes over," he says, taking another sip. Then he turns to me, appearing hesitant. "You know everything's going to be okay, right? We didn't sound as bad as I thought we would."

"I know we didn't. In fact, with a little more practice, I think we're going to be able to rock it."

"Good, because I'm worried about you. You've been distant lately." He picks at the label on the beer bottle. "I'm worried you might change your mind at the last second and not go on this tour. And I know something's going on with Ayden. You guys are always acting strange, and I saw him talking to a police officer at school the other day."

"Sage, I'm not going to change my mind about the

tour. I might be bummed Ayden isn't coming, but this has been my dream since I was like five years old and my dad taught me how to play the guitar." I shift my weight and tuck a few strands of my hair behind my ear, trying to figure out what to tell him about Ayden. "As for Ayden, you'll have to ask him what's going on. It's not my story to tell."

"Yeah, I guess I get that." He backs up toward the dance floor. "I'm going to go celebrate the beginning of what is going to be a fucking awesome journey. You should join me."

"I will in just a bit," I promise him. "I could use a fun distraction."

He grins then whirls around and dives into the mob.

I start to head for the bar to get a drink of water when my phone vibrates from my pocket. I fish it out and inch to the side of the room where it's a bit less grind-up-on-each-other so I can read the message.

**Ayden: Yep. She was awake. Sorry I missed the band play. I just got so caught up in talking to Sadie. And I really didn't want to leave.**

**Me: Don't apologize. U should be there with her.**

**Ayden: Well, I'm not there right now. The nurse kicked us out because visiting hours were over and Sadie needed to rest.**

**Me: R U home? I'll head there if you are.**

"Actually, I'm here." Ayden's voice sails over my shoulder.

A huge smile plasters across my face as I spin around and loop my arms around him. "Tell me how it went. I want to hear everything."

"I will, but let's go sit down," he says, brushing his lips across my cheek.

When I pull back, he places a hand on the small of my back and steers me toward the bar. We take a seat near the end where there are fewer people and the music isn't so loud. While Ayden asks the bartender for two cups of water, I seize the opportunity to study him, trying to determine if he looks upset or not. He actually looks pretty content, so I'm hoping the visit with his sister went well.

"I'm going to tell you what happened," he says, as if he reads my mind. "But there's something else I need to tell you first."

I pick up the glass of water the bartender sets down in front of me. "Should I be worried?"

He shakes his head, brushing a few strands of his dark hair out of his eyes. "This is actually a good thing."

"Okay." The silence is maddening as I wait for him to explain. "Ayden, please, pretty please with a cherry on top, tell me what's going on. The anticipation and build up is killing me."

He chuckles, so enjoying the slow torture he's putting me through. "Fine, but only because you pretty pleased." His fingers wrap around the glass of water, and he takes a sip before he says, "I'm going on the tour. Well, as long as you guys will take me back."

"Of course we'll take you back! I've never been so happy in my life!" I shout then roll my eyes at myself. "Well, okay, that might be a tad bit dramatic, but whatever. I'm super excited!"

He busts up laughing but then grows solemn. "I'm not going to be there the entire time. Well, I will for most of the performances, but I'm going to fly and drive back home whenever I can so I can spend time with Sadie."

"That's okay. You should spend time with her." Unable to contain my excitement, I jump onto his lap. "I'm just glad you're going."

"I am too." His hand slips around my back and urges me closer.

"You're doing this because you want to, though, right?" I ask. "Not just to make me happy. I know I've been a little whiney about you not going, but I never want you to do something you don't want to do."

"I want to go. I love playing my guitar. Plus, this is a once in a lifetime opportunity I don't want to miss out on," he says. "But I'd be lying if I didn't say that part of the reason I want to go so badly is because of you. I can't be away from you for that long. And I want to be there for you, like all the times you've been there for me."

I lean back, looking him in the eyes. "I can totally accept that answer."

"Good," he says, then casts a glance over his shoulder toward the dance floor where Sage is jumping up around and failing his hands in the air. Then he looks over at Nolan just down the bar from us, chatting with a couple of girls. "I should probably go ask Sage and Nolan if they're cool with this. You guys did find a replacement, right?"

"But we never promised him he could go on the tour with us. Tonight was like a try out." I hop off his lap and tug him to his feet. "Trust me. They're going to be stoked you're coming." I pause before I drag him over to Sage. "Everything was okay with Sadie, though, right? I mean, as okay as anything can be in that kind of situation."

He wavers, biting on his bottom lip. "I think she's okay.

Not great. I mean, I talked to her for hours, which has to mean something. But I could see the fear in her eyes, and she was really nervous around other people." He massages his chest with his hand like his heart literally aches for her. "She reminds me a lot of myself three or four years ago… And she refused to talk about anything other than me and my life… I worry she won't be able to recover from this if she doesn't deal with stuff."

"Ayden, I'm so sorry. I know it has to be hard for you to see her like that." And poor Sadie for having to go through what she has. It's such a horrible thing and I want to help her so much. Maybe I can. Maybe Ayden and I can help her get through this. "But look at you. You've changed so much since you first showed up at the Gregorys' house. If you can overcome it, I think she might be able to also."

"I just wish she didn't have such a difficult time ahead of her," he whispers, his beautiful eyes glossy with impending tears. "I think that's what makes this so hard. Me knowing how difficult it's going to be for her to heal. "

"I know… But we can be there for her. You and I… I want to help."

"I know you do, and I want you to help. She could use a friend like you even if she might not act like she does."

A smile tugs at my lips. "You mean like how you needed me?"

He nods, smoothing his thumb across my skin before he cups my cheek. "Lyric, there aren't even words to describe how lucky I am to have you in my life… If it wouldn't have been for you and your insane need to make me happy… I'm not sure I would even be here." He crushes me against his chest, hugging me tightly.

We stay that way for at least a full song, hugging each

other, savoring the moment we could've very well never had. It's such a simple thing, a hug, just arms around each other, lungs breathing, hearts beating, two people standing in the middle of tons of other people all having their own experiences. But the moment feels so epically important to me, like this is the start to something bigger—a starting point to a long, twisty, but very exciting road.

I tip my head back to meet his eyes. "How about we go celebrate this ever so amazing time we have together by telling Sage and Nolan that you're back in the band? And then we can all celebrate."

"I'm just crossing my fingers they'll want to celebrate," he says as he follows me toward the dance floor.

I end up being right. Sage and Nolan are more than thrilled to have Ayden back in the band. Sage even does his celebration dance, which basically means he makes an ass of himself by attempting to break dance.

The night ends on a perfect note. And I have a feeling there's going to be a lifetime full of them.

# Ayden

The next few weeks go by fast. Most of my days are spent packing my stuff, practicing with my band, and helping Sadie adjust to living with the Gregorys and getting to know her as much as she'll let me. She seems to be doing okay in her new life, but she spends a lot of time in her room, listening to music. Lila has her in therapy three times a week, and I think Sadie might be taking something for anxiety, even though no one has flat out said it. I'd probably be less willing to go on the tour, but I remind myself that I'll be returning home next week to visit and the week after that.

Lila and Ethan have set up flights and car rides home for me, so I'll never be gone for more than a handful of days, and Lyric is even coming home with me some of those times. While Sadie insists it's unnecessary to come home to see her, I'd never be able to live with myself if I bailed out of her life for three months. And I want to get to know her when she's ready to let me in.

It's strange to think I'll be leaving soon. That I'll be out on the road, completely free to live my life without the threat of the Soulless Mileas trying to take me. Many of the members are in jail now and are being charged with many crimes. But the most relieving part is that my father is being charged with my brother Felix's murder and my mom's, something Detective Rannali informed me of during a phone call a few days ago. He also told me that my sister and I might have to testify during the case. I wasn't too happy about that, but I'll face it when the time comes. Right now, I just want to take things one step at a time and focus on the good stuff in my life.

The day finally arrives to say bye to everyone and leave for the tour. Saying goodbye to the Gregorys is hard, but saying goodbye to Sadie is the most difficult.

"Call me if you need anything at all," I say as I hug her goodbye in the driveway.

"I will." She puts an unsteady arm around me, doing her best to hug me back. We're both extremely nervous huggers so the moment is awkward, but I'm just glad we're here to experience it.

"And I mean it. Morning, noon, and night," I say. "I'll have my phone on me at all times. I want to be there for you. No matter what you need, just call me."

"Look at you, Shy Boy," Lyric says as she swings her leg over the fence and leaps into my yard. She has on a backpack and is carrying her guitar case, ready to hit the road. "You're starting to sound like me."

"That's actually a really good compliment." I hug Sadie for a second longer then step back. "Are you sure you're going to be okay?" I ask her.

Her eyes flick back at the Gregorys' home then she nods, hugging her arms around herself. "This place seems okay." Her gaze slides to Lyric and she timidly waves.

When the two of them met, they seemed to hit it off. I wish they had more time to get to know each other before we take off, wish Sadie and I had more time too. But I remind myself that I'll be back here next week, and the week after.

"Hey, Sadie." Lyric grins as she waves. "Did you get that old guitar I sent over?"

Sadie nods then flinches as a dog starts howling from one of the neighbors' yards. "I did. Thanks for giving it to me. You didn't have to."

"I know, but I wanted to." Lyric smiles reassuringly, making Sadie the slightest bit less uneasy.

I'm not surprised Sadie seems less nervous being around Lyric. Well, less nervous than she is around other people. It was Lyric's positivity that made me feel content even in the most unsettling times, and gave me hope that one day I could be happy too. I'm crossing my fingers it'll do the same for Sadie.

"Well, thank you... I-I'm really excited to learn how to play it," Sadie says to Lyric then she nervously backs away as a SUV pulls up in the driveway. "I think I'm just going to wait on the steps." She rushes back to the porch and sinks down on the stairs, eyeballing Sage and Nolan as they get out of the car.

Nolan walks around and opens the back of the SUV while Sage strolls up the driveway toward us.

"You guys ready to get this show on the road?" Sage asks, then his gaze darts to Sadie. "Who's that?"

"That's my sister," I say, picking up my bag from off the ground.

"They adopted someone else?" Sage asks with a crook of his brow.

"Kind of," I say, not ready to tell Sage the details of my life yet.

I sling my duffel bag over my shoulder and head down the driveway to load up my stuff. After we've gotten everything into the car, Lyric says goodbye to her parents while I give everyone in my family a hug.

Once I'm finished with the goodbyes, I slide into the backseat of the SUV with Lyric. She holds my hand as Nolan backs out onto the road.

"It's kind of funny," Lyric says, resting her head on my shoulder. "But you were doing this exact same thing a couple of years ago, only you were going to the house instead of away from it. It's crazy to think about."

She's right. The day I arrived at the Gregorys' I was sitting in the backseat of their SUV, feeling nervous and alone in the world. But that lonely, scared guy who feared life and hated himself isn't the person sitting in this seat right now. I'm so much different. I have dreams now. Want things. Have people who care about me. Who love me. Who are there for me.

*I'm not alone anymore.*
*I'm not a ghost.*
*Who floats through life.*
*I'm a person*
*Who breathes the possibilities.*
*Who has hope.*

"Not everything's the same." I sit back and hold Lyric's hand, knowing this is exactly where I belong, no matter what happens.

# About the Author

## About the Author

Jessica Sorensen is a *New York Times* and *USA Today* best-selling author who lives in the snowy mountains of Wyoming. When she's not writing, she spends her time reading and hanging out with her family.

Also by Jessica Sorensen

**Unraveling You Series:**

Unraveling You

Raveling You

Awakening You

Inspiring You

Fated by Darkness

Untitled (coming soon)

**Sunnyvale Series:**

The Year I Became Isabella Anders

The Year of Falling in Love

The Year of Second Chances

The Year of Kai and Isa: Volume 1

The Year of Kai and Isa: Volume 2 (coming soon)

**Enchanted Chaos Series:**

Enchanted Chaos

Shimmering Chaos

Iridescent Chaos

Untitled (coming soon)

**Capturing Magic:**

Chasing Wishes

Chasing Magic

Untitled (coming soon)

## Chasing the Harlyton Sisters Series:

Chasing Hadley

Falling for Hadley

Holding onto Hadley

Untitled (coming soon)

## Cursed Hadley:

Cursed Hadley

Enchanting Hadley (coming soon)

## Tangled Realms:

Forever Violet: Everlasting Moonlight

Forever Stardust: Everlasting Stardust

Untitled (coming soon)

## Curse of the Vampire Queen:

Tempting Raven

Enchanting Raven

Alluring Raven

Untitled (coming soon)

## Unexpected Series:

The Unexpected Complications of Revenge

Untitled (coming soon)

## Shadow Cove Series:

What Lies in the Darkness

What Lies in the Dark

Untitled (coming soon)

## Mystic Willow Bay Series:

The Secret Life of a Witch

Broken Magic

Stolen Kisses

One Wild, Crazy Zombie Night

Magical Whispers & the Undead

Untitled (coming soon)

## Standalones:

The Forgotten Girl

## Honeyton Annabella:

The Illusion of Annabella

Untitled (coming soon)

## Rebels & Misfits:

Confessions of a Kleptomaniac

Rules of a Rebel and a Shy Girl

## The Heartbreaker Society:

The Opposite of Ordinary

The Heartbreaker Society Curse

The Heartbreaker Society Secret (coming soon)

The Secret of Ella and Micha

The Forever of Ella and Micha

The Temptation of Lila and Ethan

The Ever After of Ella and Micha

Lila and Ethan: Forever and Always

Ella and Micha: Infinitely and Always

Untitled (coming soon)

## The Shattered Promises Series:

Shattered Promises

Fractured Souls

Unbroken

Broken Visions

Scattered Ashes

Untitled (coming soon)

## Breaking Nova Series:

Breaking Nova

Saving Quinton

Delilah: The Making of Red

Nova and Quinton: No Regrets

Tristan: Finding Hope

Wreck Me

Ruin Me

Untitled (coming soon)

## The Fallen Star Series:

The Fallen Star

The Underworld

The Vision

The Promise

The Lost Soul

The Evanescence

Untitled (coming soon)

## The Darkness Falls Series:

Darkness Falls

Darkness Breaks

Darkness Fades

Untitled (coming soon)

## The Death Collectors Series (NA and YA):

Ember X and Ember

Cinder X and Cinder

Spark X and Spark

Untitled (coming soon)

## Unbeautiful Series:

Unbeautiful

Untamed

Untitled (coming soon)

Made in the USA
Coppell, TX
23 February 2020